Respected Sir

The following titles by Naguib Mahfouz
are also published by Doubleday
and Anchor Books:

THE THIEF AND THE DOGS

THE BEGINNING AND THE END

WEDDING SONG

PALACE WALK

AUTUMN QUAIL

THE BEGGAR

NAGUIB
MAHFOUZ

Respected Sir

Translated by
Dr. Rasheed El-Enany

Doubleday
New York   London   Toronto   Sydney   Auckland

Mahfouz

PUBLISHED BY DOUBLEDAY
a division of Bantam Doubleday Dell Publishing Group, Inc.
666 Fifth Avenue, New York, New York 10103

DOUBLEDAY and the portrayal of an anchor with a dolphin
are trademarks of Doubleday, a division of Bantam Doubleday Dell
Publishing Group, Inc.

This English translation was originally published in Great Britain by
Quartet Books Limited, a member of the Namara Group, in 1986. The
Doubleday edition is published by arrangement with Quartet Books
Limited.

Library of Congress Cataloging-in-Publication Data
Maḥfūẓ, Najīb, 1911–
    [Ḥaḍrat al-muḥtaram. English]
    Respected sir / Naguib Mahfouz;
    translated by Rasheed El-Enany.
    —1st Doubleday ed.
        p.   cm.
    Translation of: Ḥaḍrat al-muḥtaram.
    I. Title.
PJ7846.A46H2413   1990   89-25703
892'.736—dc20   CIP

ISBN 0-385-26479-8
ISBN 0-385-26480-1 (pbk.)

10/18/90
BT
17.95

For Wafaa, Sonia, and Nadine

Acknowledgment

I am deeply grateful to my colleague Mr. G. Balfour-Paul CMG, for his meticulous and painstaking revision of my translation, a task which he undertook with the patience and thoroughness of a scholar coupled with a poet's sensitivity for words.

Translator's Introduction

With eleven novels including the present one to his name in English translation,[1] one collection of short stories,[2] two full-fledged studies of his work in book form, an increasing number of doctoral theses, and an enormous number of articles in literary and academic periodicals (all in English), Naguib Mahfouz can rightfully claim the title of the best-known and most studied Arab novelist in the English-speaking world. This is hardly surprising, as Mahfouz enjoys a similar status in his own language, in which he has been by far the most popular serious novelist, not only in his native Egypt but all over the Arabic-speaking world, all his novels having seen several reprintings in different editions.

Born in 1911, he is the grand old man of Arabic fiction, enjoying the affection and reverence of both critics and a vast reading public. He published his first novel in 1939 and since that date has written thirty-two novels and thirteen collections of short stories. In his old age he has maintained his prolific output, producing a novel a year.

The novel genre, which can be traced back to the seventeenth and eighteenth centuries in Europe, has no prototypes in classical Arabic literature, which abounded in all kinds of narrative, though none of them could be described as a precursor of the novel as we understand the term today. The Arabic novel is thus a direct descendant of European influence and Arab scholars usually attribute the first serious attempt at writing a novel in Arabic to the Egyptian author Muhammad Husayn Haykal. The novel, called *Zaynab* after the name of its heroine, and published in 1913, told in highly romanticized terms the story of a peasant girl, victim of social convention, who withers away and finally dies of unfulfilled love. Like many first attempts, the novel suffered from many artistic flaws. Thus Haykal, a well-known author and politician of his day, shyly (he first serialized the novel in a newspaper under a pseudonym) opened the door to serious writers of his generation to try their hand at this new and suspicious art form! Soon after, writers like Taha Husayn, 'Abbas al-'Aqqad, Ibrahim al-Mazini, and Tawfiq al-Hakim were to venture into the unknown realm of fiction.

The Arabic novel, however, was to wait for yet another generation for the advent of the man who was to make it the sole mission of his life and at whose hands it was to reach maturity. Naguib Mahfouz, who was born to a middle-class family in one of the oldest quarters in Cairo, was to give expression in powerful literary metaphors, over a period of nearly half a century, to the hopes and frustrations of his nation, whose modern life has been a long act of unceasing turbulence. So much did his readers identify with his work (a great deal of which was adapted for the cinema, the theater, and television) that many of his characters became household names in Egypt and elsewhere in the Arab world. On the other hand, his work, though deeply steeped in local reality, appeals to that which is universal and permanent in human nature, as shown by the relatively good reception that his fiction has met with in English and other languages since the appearance in 1966 of his first translated novel, *Midaq Alley*.

The study of Mahfouz's output shows his fiction to have passed through four distinguishable stages. The first (1939–44) comprises three novels based on the history of ancient Egypt. Though by no means works of outstanding literary merit, they provide a useful insight into the germination of the then budding young talent. Admittedly written under the influence of Sir Walter Scott's historical romances, the last of the three, namely *The Struggle of Thebes*, is particularly interesting for the way in which the novelist brought history to bear on the present political scene at the time. Drawing on the heroic struggle of the Egyptians under their patriotic Pharaohs to expel from their country the Hyksos, the foreign invaders who had ruled it for two hundred years, the novel bore a relevance to Egyptian sociopolitical reality at the time (British occupation and a ruling aristocracy of foreign stock) that was all too obvious to be missed.

Mahfouz had meant to write a whole series of novels encompassing the full history of Pharaonic Egypt; he even did the research required for such a monumental task. In the event, and perhaps luckily for the development of the Arabic novel, he was voluntarily deflected from his intended course and the scene of his next novel, *A New Cairo* (1945), was placed in the raw reality of its day. This marks the beginning of the second stage in the novelist's career, which culminated in the publication in 1956–57 of his magnum opus, *The Cairo Trilogy*. The novels of this phase include six titles, of which three are in English translation, i.e. *Midaq Alley*, *The Beginning and the End*, and Volume I of *The Cairo Trilogy* (*Palace Walk*). In this period of his writing, the novelist studied the sociopolitical ills of his society with the full analytical power afforded him by the best techniques of realism and naturalism. What emerges from the sum total of these novels is a very bleak picture of a cross section of Egyptian urban society in the twenty or so years between the two world wars. A work which stands by itself in this phase is *The Mirage* (1948), in which Mahfouz experimented for the first and last time with writing a novel closely based on Freud's theory of psychoanalysis. For his *Trilogy*, the peak of his realist/naturalist phase, the Egyptian people will forever stand in their great novelist's debt. For without this colossal saga novel in which he gives an eyewitness account of the country's political, social, religious, and intellectual life between the two wars, that period of turmoil in their nation's life would have passed undocumented.

After writing *The Trilogy*, which met with instant wide acclaim and served to focus renewed attention on his previous work, Mahfouz fell uncharacteristically silent for a number of years (1952–59), *The Trilogy* having been completed four years before its publication. Different theories exist as to why this happened. One, endorsed by the novelist himself, is that the social reforms introduced by Nasser's revolution of 1952 made the type of social criticism he had hitherto voiced in his novels redundant. Another theory, held by Ghali Shukri,[3] a well-known Mahfouz scholar, is that by writing *The Trilogy* Mahfouz had brought the realistic technique to a point of perfection which he could not possibly surpass. He thus needed a period of incubation in which to look for a new style. Whatever the reason, when

Mahfouz serialized his next novel in the Cairo daily *al-Ahram* in 1959, his readers were in for a surprise. *The People of Our Quarter*, available in English as *Children of Gebelawi*, was a unique allegory of human history from Genesis to the present day. In it the masters of Judaism, Christianity, and Islam are stripped of their holiness and represented, in thin disguise, as no more than social reformers who strove to the best of their ability to liberate their people from tyranny and exploitation. Another character in the allegory stands for science, which is shown to have supplanted religion and at whose hands the demise of God is eventually effected. Like most of Mahfouz's novels, *Children of Gebelawi* ends on a note of gloom, though not without a flicker of hope. In this case the gloom is the corruption of *'Arafa* (science) and his alliance with the oppressive powers which finally destroy him, while the hope is in his last notebook, which contains the formulas for progress and happiness. The last scene is one of humanity frantically searching in a heap of rubbish for the promise of its salvation.

To lay down *The Trilogy* or *Children of Gebelawi* and pick up Mahfouz's next novel, *The Thief and the Dogs* (available in English), published in 1962, is, in a way, like switching from a Dickens or a Balzac to a Graham Greene or a William Golding, so radical was the change that his style underwent in the third stage of his development. No longer viewing the world through realist/naturalist eyes, he was now to write a series of short powerful novels at once social and existential in their concern. Rather than presenting a full colorful picture of society, he now concentrated on the inner workings of the individual's mind in its interaction with the social environment. In this phase his style ranges from the impressionistic to the surrealist, a pattern of evocative vocabulary and imagery binds the work together, and extensive use is made of the stream of consciousness or, to use a more accurate term in the case of Mahfouz, free indirect speech.[4] On the other hand, while the situation is based on reality, it is often given a universal significance through the suggestion of a higher level of meaning.

Just as his realistic novels were an indictment of the social conditions prevailing in Egypt before 1952, the novels of the sixties contained much that was audaciously critical of Nasser's Egypt. However, the defeat of the Arabs in the war with Israel in 1967 and its aftermath proved a shattering experience for Naguib Mahfouz from which, it would not be an invalid assumption to make, his work has never completely recovered. In the years following 1967, his writing ranged from surrealist, almost absurd short stories and dry, abstract, unactable playlets to novels of direct social and political commentary with no great literary merit, such as *Love under the Rain* (1973) and *The Karnak* (1974). Mahfouz himself was aware of the new turn his work had taken. He wanted to get his views across to the reader at a time of crisis in as simple and straightforward a way as possible; of his disposition at the time he admits to an interviewer that he was prepared to write a novel that would die the moment its occasion had passed.[5] This passionate concern of the writer for the loss of direction that his nation has suffered can be seen to have survived into the eighties in *There Only Remains One Hour* (1982), which is a kind of condensed saga novel giving an account of the

failure of successive generations of leaders and their ad-
herents to bring peace and prosperity to Egypt, and also
in *The Day the Leader Was Murdered* (1985), which de-
scribes the life of the Egyptians during the Sadat era.

In the mid-seventies we find Mahfouz again searching
for a new style. It would appear that, having been diverted
by national traumatic events from the course he had em-
barked on in the early sixties, he was no longer able to
return to it. Or it may be that in his old age, with a life's
experience behind him, he felt at last that he could Arabi-
cize the art of the novel. For it is since then that we ob-
serve the sporadic emergence of a number of novels which
justify the proposition of a fourth stage in his literary development (which has yet to be studied). What is remark-
able about the novels of this stage, of which we can count
five, is their departure from the norms of novel writing as
they evolved in Europe over the last two centuries; these
are the norms which conceive of the novel as a work of
indivisible unity which proceeds logically from a beginning
to a middle to an end. But Mahfouz no longer wants any
of that. He now harks back to the indigenous narrative arts
of Arabic literature, particularly as found in the *maqama*
form and in *The Arabian Nights* and other folk narratives in
which Arabic literature abounds. While any talk of an or-
ganic unity in these works is precluded, the presence of
what may be called, for the lack of a better term, a cu-
mulative unity producing a total effect of sorts is undeni-
able. It is this form that Mahfouz has been experimenting
with for the last ten years or so in novels like *The Epic of
the Riff-Raff*, *The Nights of "The Thousand and One Nights"*
and others. In his evocation of both the form and the con-

tent of these classical Arabic narrative types, and his utilization of them to pass judgment on the human condition past and present, Mahfouz appears to open endless vistas for the young Arab novelist to find a distinct voice of his own.

Although Mahfouz's novelistic technique has passed, as we have seen, through four recognizable stages, one cannot say the same about his worldview, the main features of which can be traced back to his earliest works. Mahfouz appears indeed to have sorted out the main questions about life at an early juncture of his youth and to have held on to the answers he arrived at ever since, age and experience serving only to deepen and broaden but hardly to modify them.

A sociopolitical view of man's existence is at the very root of almost everything that Mahfouz has written. Even in a novel with a strong metaphysical purport like *al-Tariq* (*The Way*), the social message is aptly woven into the texture of the work: man is not meant to spend his life on earth in a futile search for an apparently apathetic God and his only true hope of salvation is in the exertion of a positive and responsible effort to better his lot and that of others. That Mahfouz has always been a socially committed writer with a deep concern for the problem of social injustice is an incontestable fact. To him individual morality is inseparable from social morality. In other words, according to Mahfouz's moral code, those who only seek their own individual salvation are damned; to him nirvana is, as it were, a distinctly collective state. On the other hand, characters who are saved in Mahfouz's world are only those with altruistic motives, those who show concern for others and demonstrate a kind of awareness of their particular predicament being part of a more general one.

The picture of the world as it emerges from the bulk of Mahfouz's work is very gloomy indeed, though not completely despondent. It shows that the author's social utopia is far from being realized in his country and in the world at large. What further augments the bleakness of the human condition in Mahfouz's worldview is the fact that in addition to social oppression and the individual's moral frailty, man's toil is also thwarted by an even more destructive power: time. Mahfouz seems to conceive of time as a metaphysical force of oppression. His novels have consistently shown time as the bringer of change, and change as a very painful process, and very often time is not content until it has dealt his heroes the final blow of death. To sum up, in Mahfouz's dark tapestry of the world there are only two bright spots. These consist of man's continuing struggle for equality on the one hand and the promise of scientific progress on the other (deliverance from above is out), but meanwhile, life is a tragedy. It is interesting to listen to what the novelist himself has to say on the subject:

> As long as life ends in disability and death, it is a tragedy. As a matter of fact, the definition of tragedy applies to nothing more than it does to life ... Even those who see it as a crossroad to the hereafter will have to accept that the first part of it is a tragedy; even though it might turn out otherwise when seen in its entirety. But the tragedy of life is a complex rather than a simple one. For when we think of life as merely existence, we tend

to see it only in the abstract terms of existence and non-existence, but when we think of it as social existence, we discover in it many artificial tragedies of man's own making, such as ignorance, poverty, exploitation, violence, brutality ... etc. This justifies our emphasis on the tragedies of society, because these are tragedies that can be remedied and because in the act of remedying them we create civilization and progress. Indeed, progress might ameliorate the disaster of the original tragedy [i.e. death], and might even conquer it altogether.[6]

Like many of his novels, *Respected Sir* was first serialized in the Cairo daily *al-Ahram* and later published in book form in 1975. The novel thus pertains to Mahfouz's third stage outlined above. The story of the rise and fall of a petty government clerk, however, can in itself hardly make for compelling reading, but Mahfouz manages to make it exactly that. How he achieves this is a question for which the present translator would like to venture an answer without wishing to influence the opinion of the reader, who should perhaps refrain from reading the rest of the introduction until he has read the novel itself.

The opening passage of the novel represents anything but an objective description of the Director General's office. It is rendered in highly inflated prose which clearly reflects the magnitude of the impression it makes on the protagonist. In other words, the language here is psychological rather than realistic and its terms of reference lie almost solely within the character's mind rather than in the real world outside. This hyperbolic use of language characterizes the prose of the whole novel and is found on almost every page of it. Thus while the experience of the novel is a fairly mundane one mainly portraying the rise and fall of a self-made, ego-centered careerist, it is told in extremely heightened language. The vocabulary used in the extract above and throughout the novel is religious. It is deliberately used by the author to transfer what is essentially a prosaic experience to a much higher plane. Thus, throughout, the protagonist's professional ambition is presented in vocabulary and imagery which evoke an exalted and arduous religious quest, as though the attainment of the position of Director General were a sacred mission, ordained by divine will, for the sake of which no sacrifice was too dear.

To what effect, then, does Mahfouz swap linguistic registers, i.e. the exalted for the mundane? The answer is: irony. Mahfouz creates an intricate pattern of verbal irony which he weaves into the very texture of the novel and maintains throughout. This pattern of verbal irony engenders in the reader an awareness of the incongruity between the object and mode of expression, i.e. the realistic situation and the hyperbolic terms in which it is rendered. This awareness creates and sustains, all the way through, a sense of dramatic irony where the reader is, as it were, cognizant of a basic fact of which the protagonist is ignorant, namely that his obsession has misguided him, that there is nothing holy about his ambition, and that, in his quest for salvation, he has only fallen into a hell of his own making. It is in the creation and sustainment of this pattern of verbal irony and in the complete subjugation of the novelistic experience to a language order originally alien to it that Mahfouz has, in the opinion of the present writer, achieved a feat unprecedented not only in his own work but probably in Arabic fiction altogether.

NOTES

1. The other ten are:
   Midaq Alley, Khayat, Beirut, 1966; corrected edition: Heinemann, London, 1975
   Mirrors, Bibliotheca Islamica, Chicago, 1977
   Miramar, Heinemann, 1978
   Children of Gebelawi, Heinemann, 1981
   Wedding Song, Doubleday/Anchor Books, 1989
   The Thief and the Dogs, Doubleday/Anchor Books, 1989
   The Beginning and the End, Doubleday/Anchor Books, 1989
   Autumn Quail, Doubleday/Anchor Books, 1990
   The Cairo Trilogy, Volume I, *Palace Walk*, Doubleday, 1990
   The Beggar, Doubleday/Anchor Books, 1990
2. *God's World: An Anthology of Short Stories*, Bibliotheca Islamica, Minneapolis, 1973
3. See his book on Mahfouz, *al-Muntami* (*The Conformist*), Cairo, 1969
4. For a discussion of this issue see the translator's doctoral thesis, *Hadrat al-Muhtaram by Naguib Mahfouz: a Translation and a Critical Assessment*, University of Exeter, 1984, pp. 206–9
5. See Naguib Mahfouz, *Atahaddath Ilaykum* (*I Speak to You*), Beirut, 1977, p. 111.
6. Ibid., pp. 73–74.

Respected Sir

ONE

The door opened to reveal an infinitely spacious room: a whole world of meanings and motivations, not just a limited space buried in a mass of detail. Those who entered it, he believed, were swallowed up, melted down. And as his consciousness caught fire, he was lost in a magical sense of wonder. At first, his concentration wandered. He forgot what his soul yearned to see—the floor, the walls, the ceiling: even the god sitting behind the magnificent desk. An electric shock went through him, setting off in his innermost heart an insane love for the gloriousness of life on the pinnacle of power. At this point the clarion call of power urged him to kneel down and offer himself in sacrifice. But he followed, like the rest, the less extreme path of pious submissiveness, of subservience, of security. Many childlike tears he would have to shed before he could impose his will. Yielding to an irresistible temptation, he cast a furtive glance at the divinity hunched behind the desk and lowered his eyes with all the humility he possessed.

Hamza al-Suwayfi, the Director of Administration, led in the procession.

"These are the new employees, Your Excellency," he said, addressing the Director General.

The Director General's eyes surveyed their faces, including his. He felt he was becoming part of the history of government and that he stood in the divine presence. He thought he heard a strange whispering sound. Perhaps he alone heard it. Perhaps it was the voice of Destiny itself. When His Excellency had completed his examination of their faces, he opened his mouth. He spoke in a quiet and gentle voice, revealing little or nothing of his inner self.

"Have they all got the Secondary Education Diploma?" he inquired.

"Two of them have the Intermediate Diploma of Commerce," Hamza al-Suwayfi replied.

"The world is progressing," said the Director General in an encouraging tone. "Everything is changing. And now here is the Diploma, replacing the Certificate of Primary Education."

This was reassuring, but they all sought to conceal their delight under still greater submissiveness.

"Live up to what's expected of you," His Excellency went on, "through hard work and honesty."

He looked over a list of their names and suddenly asked, "Which of you is Othman Bayyumi?"

Othman's heart pounded within him. That His Excellency had uttered his very own name shook him to the core. Without raising his eyes he took a step forward and mumbled, "Me, Your Excellency."

"You got an excellent grade in your Diploma. Why didn't you go on to finish your education?"

In his confusion he remained silent. The fact was he did not know what to say, even though he knew the answer.

The Director of Administration answered for him, apologetically, "Perhaps it was his circumstances, Your Excellency."

Again he heard that strange whispering, the voice of Destiny. And for the first time he felt a sensation of blue skies and of a strange but pleasant fragrance pervading the room. The reference to his "circumstances" was no worry to him, now that he had been sanctified by His Excellency's kindly and appreciative notice. He thought to himself that he could take on a whole army and vanquish it all alone. Indeed his spirit soared upward, higher and higher, till his head disappeared into the clouds in a surge of wild intoxication. But His Excellency tapped the edge of the desk and said, by way of ending the interview, "Thank you. Good morning."

Othman went out of the room, silently reciting the Throne verse from the Qur'an.

TWO

I am on fire, O God.

Flames were devouring his soul from top to bottom as it soared upward into a world of dreams. In a single moment of revelation he perceived the world as a surge of dazzling light which he pressed to his bosom and held on to like one demented. He had always dreamed and desired and yearned, but this time he was really ablaze, and in the light of this sacred fire he glimpsed the meaning of life.

But down on earth it was decided that he should join the Archives Section. It did not matter how he started; life itself evolved from a single cell or perhaps from something even less. He descended to his new abode in the basement of the ministry, his wings still fluttering. He was greeted by gloom and the musty smell of old paper. Outside, through a barred window, he saw that the ground was on the same level as his head. Inside, the huge room spread out in front of him. Rows of filing cabinets stood on either side, and another long row divided the room down the middle. Staff desks were placed in gaps between cabinets. He walked behind one of the employees toward a desk at the front placed crosswise in a recess like a prayer niche. At the desk was seated the Head of the Archives Section. Othman had not yet recovered from the upsurge of divine inspiration. Even his descent into the basement could not wake him up. He walked behind the clerk, perplexed, distracted, and excited.

"Man's aspirations are infinite," he said to himself.

The clerk introduced him to the Head of Section: "Mr. Othman Bayyumi, the new clerk," he said, and then introduced the Section Head to him: "Our chief, Mr. Sa'fan Basyuni."

He recognized something familiar in the man's features, as if he were a native of his own alley. He liked the protruding bones of his face, its dark and taut skin and the white, disheveled hair of his head. He liked even more the kind and friendly look in his eyes which strove in vain to reflect an air of authority. The man smiled, revealing his ugliest feature: black teeth with wide gaps in between them.

"Welcome to the Archives Section! Sit down!" he said, and started to shuffle through the documents of his appointment.

"Welcome! Welcome! Life," he went on to say, "can be summed up in two words: hello and goodbye." Yet it was infinite, Othman thought. There blew around him a strange mysterious wind, full of all kinds of probabilities.

It was infinite, he thought again, and because of that it demanded infinite willpower.

The Head of Section pointed to a vacant, neutral-colored desk whose leather top was worn-out and spotted with faded stains of ink.

"Your desk," he said. "Examine the chair carefully. The tiniest nail can rip a new suit."

"My suit is very old anyway," replied Othman.

"And remember," the man carried on with his warning, "to recite a prayer before opening a filing cabinet. On the eve of last Bairam festival a snake, at least three feet long, came out of one of the cabinets." He choked with laughter and continued, "But it wasn't a poisonous one."

"How can one tell whether it is poisonous or not?" asked Othman anxiously.

"You ask the section messenger. He comes from Abu Rawwash, the city of snakes."

Othman took the warning for a joke and let it pass. He chided himself for failing to study meticulously His Excellency the Director General's room and print on his mind's eye a full picture of the man's face and his person, for not trying to unravel the secret of the magic with which he dominated everyone and had them at his beck and call. This was the power to be worshipped. It was the ultimate beauty too. It was one of the secrets of the universe. On earth there existed divine secrets without number for those who had eyes to see and minds to think. The time between hello and goodbye was short. But it was infinite as well. Woe betide anyone who ignored this truth. There were people who never moved, like Mr. Sa'fan Basyuni. Well-meaning but miserable, paying tribute to a wisdom of which he had learned nothing. But not so those whose hearts had been touched by the sacred fire. There was a happy path which began at the eighth grade in the government service and ended at the splendid position of His Excellency the Director General. This was the highest ideal available to the common people, beyond which they could not aspire. This was the highest heaven where both divine mercy and human pride became manifest. The eighth grade. The seventh. The sixth. The fifth. The fourth. The third. The second. The first. Director General. The miracle could be brought about in thirty-two years. Or perhaps rather more. Those who fell by the wayside were innumerable. Still the celestial order did not necessarily apply to mankind, least of all to government employees. Time nestled in his arms like a gentle child, but one could not prophesy one's future. He was on fire: that was all. And it seemed to him that this fire blazing in his breast was the same as that which lit the stars in their courses. We were creatures of mystery whose secrets were hidden to all but their Creator.

"You will first learn to handle the incoming mail," said Mr. Basyuni. "It is easier." He then added, laughing, "An archivist should take off his jacket while working. Or at least have elbow patches sewn on his sleeves to protect them against dust and paper clips." All that was easy. What was really difficult was how to deal with time.

THREE

In his one-room flat he could subject himself to scrutiny. There, the meaning of his life took shape before him. He lived with his senses always on the alert and with heightened awareness, constantly seeking to provide himself with every possible weapon. From his small window he could see the place where he was born: al-Husayni Alley, an extension of his body and soul. A long back street with a sharp bend, famous for its parking area for carts and its watering trough for donkeys. The house where he had been born and brought up had been demolished. In its place there was now a little plot for pushcarts. Few of the natives of the alley ever left it for good except for the grave. They went to work in various quarters: al-Mabyada, al-Darrasa, al-Sikka al-Jadida, or even beyond, but they came back at the end of the day. One of the characteristics of the alley was that it knew no murmurs or whispers. Voices here were very loud, sometimes crude, sometimes full of wisdom. Among them was one very close to him, a strong, coarse voice which age had not weakened, the voice of Omm Husni, the landlady. Dreams of eternity were wearisome indeed. But what had he been yesterday, and what was he today? He would do well not to recoil from the impossible. He would do well not to surrender himself to the current without a definite plan. An exact plan. He often dreamed that he was urinating, but always

woke up at the right moment. What did that mean? Omm
Husni had been a workmate of his mother's. A lifetime
friend and confidante. Both were married to cart drivers
and both had slaved away with the patience and persis-
tence of ants for a few piastres with which to help their
husbands and keep their homes together. They had
worked as peddlers, hairdressers, marriage brokers, and so
on. His mother was still working when she died. As for
Omm Husni, she went on slaving away with great zeal.
She had more luck and earned more than his mother and
thus was able to save up enough money to build her three-
story house: a timber store on the ground floor and two
flats above. She lived in one and Othman in the other. As
for her son Husni, the days of war and hardship had led
him to distant lands where he settled down, and all he had
left behind was his name.

Did he not have the right to dream? Dream he did,
thanks to the holy flame burning in his breast. Thanks to
his small room too. He got used to his dreams just as he
got used to the bed, the settee, the chest, the mat, and, for
that matter, the sound of his own voice, sometimes shrill,
sometimes melodious, which echoed against the dark, solid
walls.

What had he been yesterday? His father had wanted to
make of him a cart driver like himself, but the sheikh of
the local Qur'an school said to him, "Put your trust in
God, Mr. Bayyumi, and enroll the boy at the primary
school."

His father did not seem to comprehend.

"Has he not learned enough Qur'an for him to perform
the prayers?" he asked.

"The boy is clever and intelligent. One day he could make a civil servant," replied the sheikh.

Mr. Bayyumi guffawed incredulously.

"Try the charity schools. He might be accepted free," the sheikh said.

Mr. Bayyumi had hesitated for a while, but eventually the miracle took place. At school Othman achieved astonishing success until he finally obtained the Primary Certificate. He drew ahead of his barefooted playmates from the alley and was acutely aware of the first holy spark from his throbbing heart. He was certain that God had blessed his footsteps and that the gates of infinity lay open before him. He joined a secondary school, also free, and achieved greater success than anyone in al-Husayni Alley could believe. But when he was still in the second form, his father contracted a terminal illness. He felt miserable at what he had "done" to his son.

"I am leaving you behind a helpless schoolboy," he said to him. "Who will drive the cart? Who will provide for the family?"

His father died a sad man. But his mother worked twice as hard, hoping that God would make a great man of her son. Was not God all-powerful? If it had not been for the unexpected death of his mother, Othman would have completed his higher education. His anguish was great, all the more so because of his heightened awareness of his ambition and the sacred aspirations throbbing within him. Sacred too was the memory of his parents. And on every religious occasion he would visit their grave, a paupers' grave which lay in an open piece of land amid a host of the forgotten. Now he was alone. A branch cut off a tree. His elder brother, who had been a policeman, had been killed in a demonstration. His sister had died of typhoid in the fever hospital. Another brother had died in prison. The memory of his family was painful to him, and how he mourned for his parents! He linked these happenings with an exalted drama which he contemplated with respect and awe. For fortunes were determined in the alley through conflicting wills and unknown forces and then consecrated in eternity. By this token his belief in himself was boundless, though in the end he depended on Almighty God. And for the same reason he would never miss a prayer, least of all the Friday service at al-Husayn Mosque. Like the people of his alley, he made no distinction between religion and life. Religion was for life and life for religion, and a glittering jewel like the position of Director General was only a sacred station on the divine and infinite path. Living among his colleagues with his senses alert and shining, he picked up the sort of ideas and maxims that seemed important to him. He then devoted himself to laying out a precise plan for the future, which he translated into a working schedule to be studied every morning before going out to work:

Program for Work and Living
1. fulfillment of duties with care and honesty;
2. study of the Financial Bill as if it were a holy book;
3. studying for a university degree as an external student;
4. a special study of English and French, as well as Arabic;

5. acquisition of general knowledge, particularly of the kind beneficial to a civil servant;
6. demonstration, by every proper means, of piety and rectitude as well as diligence in work;
7. efforts to gain the confidence and friendship of seniors;
8. seizing useful opportunities without the sacrifice of self-respect. For instance: helping out someone in a position of influence, making useful friendships or a happy marriage conducive to progress.

He often looked at a small mirror which was nailed to the wall between the window and the clothes stand to examine his appearance and reassure himself on this point. Certainly his appearance would not be an obstacle. He was well built like the people of his alley. He had a dark, longish face with a high, clear forehead and well-trimmed hair. On the whole, his physique would qualify him to fill any position, no matter how important.

He drew courage and strength from the depths of his soul and thought to himself: Not a bad start—and the road is endless.

FOUR

The tryst on the edge of the wasteland was also sacred. He hastened to it with ardent heart and with the gaiety of one who has cast aside the heavy weight of life's burden. There on the skirt of the desert stood the ancient, abandoned fountain at the foot of whose steps they would sit side by side in the infinite bosom of the afternoon. Before them the desert stretched as far as the foot of the mountain and silence would sing in its unknown tongue. Her dark brown color resembled that of the tense evening, a hue inherited from an Egyptian mother and a Nubian father who died when she was six. Their old companionship in the alley reached back into the remote past until it vanished into the very spring of life. When he looked into her big, wide eyes or saw her small, firm body brimming with vitality, he felt himself in the presence of an ideal which excited his whole being and awakened in his instincts a kind of humble yearning. She was his childhood friend in the alley and on the roof. Although hardly sixteen, she was considered a good housewife. In fact, she had been her mother's only helper after all her seven sisters had married.

Sayyida smiled. Her face was always smiling, her eyes radiant and her limbs constantly moving with a sort of restless grace. Tresses of her thick, curly hair danced in the dry breeze coming down from the mountain. The silence was sweet. Breaking out of it she said, "My mother is pleased that you have joined the civil service . . ."

"And you?" he asked teasingly.

Her smile grew bigger, but she did not reply. He put his arm around her and their lips met, hers full, his sharply defined. No mention of love had been made between them, but whenever they were alone together they expressed it through kisses and embraces. She satisfied in him that aspect of his soul which craved the simple pleasures of life. He also loved her with his mind because he appreciated her virtues and her sincerity and had an instinctive feeling that she could make him happy.

"You are now a government employee . . ." Her voice disclosed her admiration and he kissed her again. "No one in our alley has ever achieved that," she added.

All his friends worked in various manual trades. They watched him go by, whenever he passed, with admiration, and sometimes with envy. This would have pleased him had he not been acutely and bitterly aware of the long and difficult path ahead of him.

"You are the only white-collar worker!"

"Outside our alley that's worth nothing," he said quietly.

"Outside doesn't matter. Our alley's just a place for carts!"

He kissed her for the third time and said, "Never speak of carts without respect . . ."

"Well said! You are so noble . . ."

Her father had been arrested in the same brawl as his own brother. He went to jail, where he died of his injuries. However, these happenings were considered among the glories which made the good name of the alley. But Sayyida obviously had only one thing on her mind and it was no use ignoring it. There she was, asking the question: "And what next?"

He was aware of her yearning for a word that would set her heart at ease and make her happy. He knew too that on no account would his happiness be less than hers; it might even be greater. He loved that girl as she loved him and could not do without her. But he was afraid. He had to think a thousand times. He needed to refer to the bitter Work Program. He still had to ponder a long while on the life that lay before him, welcoming him and challenging him at the same time.

"What do you mean, Sayyida?"

"Nothing!" she answered lightly, but with an undertone of insistence.

"We shouldn't forget we are young . . ."

"Me?" She said this with mild protest, hinting sweetly at the womanhood that cried aloud within her. "Grow your mustache. That's what you need."

He took her jest seriously and thought the idea could be of real help to him in his struggle. For who could imagine a senior official without a mustache?

"I will carry on with my education, Sayyida," he said quietly.

"Do you need more education still?"

"A university degree."

"What for?"

"A useful asset for promotion."

"Will it take you long?"

"Four years, at least."

With concealed anguish, he noticed an expression of coldness in her eyes, perhaps also of shame, with something of anger in it too.

"And what do you need promotion for?"

He laughed and kissed her hair but did not dare go beyond that. The scent of her hair reminded him of childhood games and a punch in the back when they were caught playing bride and groom. The darkness of night loomed over the hilltop and a sound of singing came from a distant gramophone.

"It seems promotion is more important than I imagined . . ."

He took her hand in his and murmured, "I will love you forever . . ."

What he said was the truth, a truth accompanied by a sense of dejection and grief; and he hated himself. He said to himself that life was a grand and awesome experience, but tiresome.

FIVE

He stood at his parents' grave, lost among other countless graves, and recited the opening verse of the Qur'an. Then he said, "God have mercy upon you . . ."

Next he whispered to them in a spirit of gratitude, "Othman is now a respectable government employee taking his first steps on a difficult path, but he is resolved to follow it to the end." He bowed slightly and added with humility, "All the good things I have I owe to the Lord and to you . . ."

A blind boy was reciting some of the shorter chapters of the Qur'an. He gave him a half-piastre. Yet, insignificant as the amount was, he still had that feeling of resentment which always possessed him when he gave someone money. When the boy was gone, he addressed his parents again: "Before God I vow to move you to a new grave when He has made my wishes come true . . ."

He had no idea how much of their dead bodies would remain with the passage of time, but he reckoned that there would be something remaining at any rate. To his surprise his thoughts reverted to Sayyida, and her smiling image took shape before his eyes. It seemed to him that she was on the verge of passing some pointed remark, outspoken and sarcastic. His heart contracted with pain and he murmured, "Guide me, O God, onto the straight path, for all I do is done at Your inspiration."

He lived once again his father's last days. There was no escape from this. Sickness and old age had crippled him till his only recreation was to sit on a sheepskin in front of the house, hardly able to see or hear. He would contemplate his helplessness, crying aloud in his grief, "O Lord, have mercy . . ."

In his day, he had been counted among the strong men of the alley. Throughout his long life he had relied on the muscles of his arms and legs, toiling without a break and enduring to the end a harsh and poverty-stricken existence. His strength, which had nothing to nourish it, had been wasted; and in his misery he would break into a cackle of laughter, without meaning or reason. One evening he was found dead where he customarily sat on the sheepskin. So no one ever knew how death had come to him or how he had met it. As for his mother, her death was even more shocking. She had been doing the washing when suddenly she had bent over and begun to scream in terrible pain. An ambulance had come and carried her to Qasr al-'Ayni Hospital, where she died during an operation for appendicitis.

His family was singularly victimized by death. Something inside told him that, for this reason, perhaps he himself would live long, and a wave of sorrow swept over him. Every manner of death was reasonable compared with his brother the policeman's: a man big as an ox killed by the brickbats of the demonstrators. What a death! He had not known who they were nor had they known who he was. Othman regarded what had happened with the eyes of a spellbound spectator. It made absolutely no sense to him. True, he learned a lot from the perusal of history; he knew about history from the most ancient times up to the eve of the Great War. He knew about revolutions, but he had never lived them or reacted to them. He had seen and heard about things, but always kept aloof and wondering. No common sympathy had ever gripped his heart to draw him to the battleground; and he was always bewildered at the way groups of eminent statesmen and their supporters fought each other. He had been hounded all his life by poverty and hunger, and this had left him no time to extend the range of his thought to the outside world. The alley shut him in, its preoccupations unknown to everyone else, savage, violent, unending. Today, he was conscious of one goal only, a goal at once sacred and profane, which had nothing to do, as far as he could see, with the strange events that took place in the name of politics. He told himself that man's true life was his inner life, which governed his every heartbeat and which called for toil, dedication, and enterprise. It was something holy, something religious, and through it he could achieve self-fulfillment in the service of the sacred apparatus known as the Government or the State. Through it the glory of man was accomplished on earth, and through man God's will was accomplished on high. People applauded other, indeed quite contrary, things; but these people were foolish and fraudulent. So he never forgave himself for not having secured a full view of the Director General's room and of his singular personality which set the entire administration in motion from behind a screen—in precise order and perfect sequence, recalling to the ignorant the stars in their courses and the wisdom of heaven. He sighed deeply. He recited the *Fatiha* once more and said by way of farewell, "Pray for me, Father!" He moved around the grave, whose two headstones had fallen and whose corner had cracked, and said, "Pray for me, Mother!"

SIX

How wonderful is the turning year. He lived through its seasons, working without pause. Winter in the alley was pretty severe but it spurred a man to work; spring with its sandy khamsin wind was a curse, summer an inferno, and autumn a mysterious, meditative smile. He kept on working with an iron will and a burning passion. His law books were ranged under the bed and on the windowsill. He spent little of the night in sleep. He embraced ideas and wrestled with the inscrutable. Success alone was not enough to satisfy him. Friday was usually set aside for acquiring general knowledge worthy of directors and those in their service. He paid special attention to poetry and learned plenty of it by heart. He even tried composing it but failed. He told himself that poetry had always been the best means of currying favor with superiors and of shining at official parties. It was a heavy loss not to be able to write poetry. Still, learning it was at any rate the best way to perfect one's prose. The art of public speaking was no less important for success than poetry, and eloquence was essential, so his heart told him. Even more so were foreign languages. All these branches of knowledge were useful, and there comes a time when their value goes up in the stock exchange of officialdom. For a civil servant did not live by financial regulations alone. Indeed, he must equip himself with a measure of everything useful, for who knew what might happen? He would tell himself that his life was an unbroken stream flowing in the direction of light and learning, loaded with its cargo of all sorts of novelties and fed by tributaries from the fields of thought: a stream carried forward by the intensity of faith, nobility, and human pride to reach in the end its estuary at the divine threshold.

As for peace of mind, that he attained on the steps of the ancient fountain, in the embrace of fervid love, in the arms of the pretty, loving girl, and her burning, virgin bosom. He allowed himself no commitment in word or deed. Yet he was as fond of her as of life itself. If only life could be satisfied with love and simple happiness, he thought. So anxious was Sayyida that she cast off her natural reserve. She no longer shrank from expressing her true emotions, or revealing the ardor of her yearning for him. On one occasion she said to him in a tone of reverence, "I cannot live without you."

But her words were tepid compared with the generosity of her full lips. On another occasion she said, "You are everything to me: the past and the future . . ."

Her brown eyes glowed with fidelity, with apprehension, and with real yearning. And in the melting moment of a passionate embrace she sighed, "We lack something . . ."

"Our perfect love lacks nothing," was his dull and selfish answer.

She shrugged her shoulders in protest, while seeking not to embarrass him. She thought it better to be patient with him and to persevere.

He found that he suffered from a fearful repression that could eventually place him at the mercy of the unknown.

Thus he yielded to the temptation of a colleague who invited him to visit the official prostitutes' quarter. As one
of the breed of al-Husayni Alley, he did not lack the necessary courage. He walked ahead into a lane lit by two gas
lamps standing wide apart and covered in so thick a layer
of dust that the lane was sunk in that semi-darkness which
arouses desire; and he looked excitedly from place to place
until his eyes settled on a prey. Those visits were usually
followed by a wholehearted plea for forgiveness and a pro-
longed resort to prayer and worship, the sort of thing he
habitually did each time he faced up to his deeply hidden
intentions toward Sayyida. Thus in addition to the hardship of continuous work, he suffered even harsher hardship from the pangs of conscience. His long exhausting
nights would terminate in severe mental fatigue, almost to
the point of fainting. And sometimes tears would come to
his eyes almost without his realizing it.

Sa'fan Basyuni, the Head of Archives, watched his work
with both admiration and misgiving. He appreciated his
perseverance, discretion, and good manners. But from the
start he was uneasy about his Secondary Education Diploma, which set him apart in the Archives Section, and
also about his ambition for further education that would
raise Othman even higher above his own solitary Certificate of Primary Education. Othman became aware of this
quite quickly but he counted on the man's good nature and
redoubled his efforts to ingratiate himself with him and
comply with his every direction until Sa'fan fully trusted
him and opened his heart to him with rare candor. Thus
in his spare time he would draw closer to Othman and
speak his mind openly. Even in politics he disclosed his

views and inclinations to him. So zealous was the man that Othman shrank from ignoring his interests or declaring his own cold neutrality toward them.

"The truth is," he would say with wary ambiguity, "we are of the same turn of mind . . ."

Such words pleased the man in a way that Othman could not comprehend. The man's involvement in such things amazed him. And more amazing was the involvement of his wretched colleagues. What was it that they found attractive in them? Had they not more basic worries to occupy their minds? But he told himself with no little scorn that they were people without a fixed aim in life, that their religious faith was only superficial and that they never thought enough of the meaning of life or of what God had created them for. Thus their thoughts and their lives were wasted in empty amusement and sophistry and their true potentialities were dissipated without achievement. Illusions deceived them and they stood idle as time went by.

SEVEN

One day, after receiving the incoming mail from him, Sa'fan Basyuni said, "Come and spend an evening at my place. You'll enjoy it." Despite some surprise and misgiving he did not think of declining. The man went on: "Our neighbors are having a wedding party. We'll have an ox head for supper together and sit on the balcony to listen to the singing . . ."

He lived in a flat on the third floor of a block in al-Bahr Close in the Bab al-Sha'riyya quarter. Othman found that he was the only person invited and felt gratified by the honor that his chief bestowed on him alone. They had together a delicious supper which consisted of ox tongue, brain, cheek, and eye, along with sausage, bready beef soup, and fried onions in addition to radishes and pickles, as well as melon for dessert. It was a superb and bountiful meal and he ate his fill. They sat on a balcony overlooking the courtyard of the house where the wedding took place. The courtyard was brightly lit by numerous pressure lamps. Inside were rows of chairs and sofas packed with guests. The gangways thronged with boys and younger children while scores of others pressed around the outside fence. Lights shone inside the house as well and women were seen coming and going. The whole place reverberated with voices of every pitch and kind; bursts of laughter and coughing as well as cries of joy resounded in the air.

Othman was stirred by the wedding's air of happiness and its heartwarming scents of sexuality and love. When the band struck up, he found it more moving than he expected or was accustomed to, for he did not like music particularly, though it was all right when it came his way. Indeed, music was not all that bad sometimes. It was something good and comforting. Marriage was a splendid relationship, a joy and a religious duty. A deep splendid sadness came over him.

"Perhaps you need some fun. That's what I keep telling myself . . ." So spoke Sa'fan, looking in his direction, his face partly lit by the wedding lights, partly hidden in shadow. "Your days are slipping by in work and study, but life demands much more of us than that," he added.

He pretended to listen attentively but inside he felt contempt. He despised homilies which encouraged indolence and considered them a blasphemy against God. At the same time his thoughts returned to Sayyida in her long agony, to the duties he must fulfill and the facts he must bear in mind and reconsider. He felt a meaningless smile on his face. Sa'fan started talking again. "You are a man of high ambition, but peace of mind is a precious possession too . . ."

"You are very wise, Mr. Basyuni . . ." he said, his contempt rising.

At the doorway of the balcony a shadow appeared. It was a girl carrying a tray from which rose the aroma of mint tea. Lights from the wedding below were reflected on her face, revealing some of her features in spite of the darkness of the room behind her. She had a pale round face, evidently attractive but its charms were veiled in

mystery. He felt apprehensive. As he bent slightly forward
to pick up his cup, he saw from close up the smooth tender
skin of her arm and felt as if the scent of mint emanated
from it. She was hardly there for a minute before disap-
pearing into the darkness, the smile that had nearly escaped her timorously concealed. Silence reigned like a
feeling of guilt, the atmosphere charged with a sense of
conspiracy. His apprehension heightened.

"My daughter . . ." said Sa'fan. Othman nodded respect-
fully.

"She'd completed her primary education before she
stopped going to school." He nodded again, this time in
admiration. The voices of the group accompanying the
singer were wafted up to them. Sa'fan went on: "Home is
the real school for a girl." He did not comment. He did
not know what to say. At the same time he was annoyed
at his own silence.

"What's your view on the subject?"

"I agree with you completely."

Yet he recollected his mother's life of bitter struggle. He
felt he was being pushed into a trap. The soloist began to
sing in a soft, gentle voice. Sa'fan murmured, "How beautiful!"

"Indeed."

"Life is beautiful too."

"Absolutely."

"But it demands wisdom from us if we're to enjoy its
sweetness."

"Isn't wisdom difficult to attain?"

"No. It's a gift from God."

God did not create us for a life of ease or the taking of

shortcuts. The man was laying siege to him, but he was not going to give in. Yet how could he keep his freedom and gain his chief's favor at the same time? He no longer listened to the music. But Sa'fan went on listening, keeping time with his hands and feet and occasionally casting an inquiring look at him. He concluded that, by way of self-defense, he had better repay his invitation with one even more generous—a conclusion that caused him no slight pain. For he would never spend a single piastre except to meet a pressing need, and on the very day he received his first salary he opened a deposit account with the post office. It never occurred to him to change the place where he lived or the food he ate. He believed that thrift was an important element in his long struggle as well as a religious duty. It was also a safeguard against fear in a fearful world. Yet what must be must be. He would repay the treat with a more generous one. Moreover, it would be in a restaurant, not in his room, jam-packed with books as it was and poor in everything else. As a result, he would be spending a positively enormous amount of money. A curse on all stupid people! The sounds of music turned into a meaningless din and the gates of hell flew open. Yet the old man swayed his head to the tunes, oblivious of the offense he was committing. The world was inflicting on Othman another of its mockeries.

EIGHT

Before the end of the month, he had treated the man to dinner at al-Kashif restaurant. They had delectable fish and dessert. The old man was so happy he looked as if he expected an angel of mercy and joy to descend from heaven.

"What about spending the rest of the evening at al-Fishawi's café?" he suggested, apparently not satisfied with the dinner alone.

Othman's heart throbbed painfully, but he took his arm and said, "What a wonderful idea!"

As they sat in the café he remembered a Bairam festival in the past when his new galabiya was torn in a brawl in al-Husayni Alley. His father later gave him a beating and he had to wear the galabiya for a whole year, patched up by his mother. The old man's joviality irritated him. It was obvious he expected to hear good news. He sat there with a glow of expectation in his drab eyes and an air of general satisfaction.

"Are you happy with your colleagues in the Archives?" he said.

"Yes. I believe I am."

"They are a poor lot, but good-natured enough."

"Yes. Yes, indeed."

"As for you, you are an excellent young man. Will you become a barrister when you've got your degree?"

"No. But I hope to better my position."

"A good idea. I admire your high ambition."

Othman abandoned his hesitancy, determined to escape even if it meant stifling the man's hopes.

"My cares are greater than you imagine," he said.

The man looked at him apprehensively and said, "Heaven protect us! What's the matter?"

"It's not ambition I care about as you think. My concerns are of a humbler kind."

"Really?"

"If circumstances weren't so difficult, I would desire nothing more simple or natural than marriage."

The old man failed to disguise the disappointment which choked him. "What sort of circumstances, if I may ask?" he said.

"Huge responsibilities." Othman sighed wistfully. "People like me, brought up in poverty, cannot escape its grip ..." With bowed head he added in a voice of melancholy, "How I wish ..."

He fell silent as if overcome by emotion. The old man leaned back out of the lamplight till he was in shadow. Othman could not retract what he had said but he must preserve the man's friendship as best he could. Out of the shadow the man's voice came to him: "And when will you be able to stand on your own feet?"

"I have small children and widows to look after," he said in a tone of despair. "I'm just an ox tied blindfold to a waterwheel."

Everything went dead. Even the banging of backgammon pieces was no longer audible. He murmured again, "How I wish ..."

The old man did not utter a word. He wanted to pay the bill but Othman would not let him. He paid out of his own pocket, feeling utterly miserable. All enjoyment had gone from the party and no pretense could revive it. They left the café and walked up to Bab al-Sha'riyya Square, where the man took his leave and went off toward his home.

Othman was left in a wretched state of nervous tension. A surge of lunatic rashness swept over him, driving him to desperate extravagance of a suicidal nature.

Without wavering he made his way to the prostitutes' quarter, where he could bury his tensions and sorrows and his pangs of conscience.

"Even the sins of man must be hallowed," he said to himself in his misery.

NINE

Omm Husni stopped him as he was going downstairs. She would not do that without a good reason. He looked at her face furrowed with wrinkles, her hair dyed with henna, and her body still strong in spite of her old age. It made him think of his mother, and he shook her hand smiling.

"I've got news," she said.

"I hope it's good news."

Narrowing her single eye (the other one she had lost in a fight in the alley), she said, "There's nothing good in it."

He looked at her intently.

"A suitor. There's now a suitor standing in your way."

"Eh?"

"Somebody has proposed to Sayyida."

A sense of grief and bafflement overwhelmed him as if the news was something he could not have expected. He was lost for words.

"A tailor."

He knew this was something inevitable. He would not try to prevent it nor could he hope to. It was like death. He did not utter a word. She dragged him by the hand to her room and seated him on the settee next to herself.

"Don't you care?"

He felt a sharp pain in the depth of his soul. It was as if the world was fading away. He said angrily, "Don't ask meaningless questions!"

"Calm down!"

"I'd better go."

"But you won't be able to meet her."

The world faded more and more.

She went on: "You should have realized that by yourself."

"How do you mean?"

"Her mother is keeping a strict eye on her movements. A real man is better than an illusion ..."

"A real man is better than an illusion," he mumbled in a stupor.

"You love her, don't you?"

"I love her," he said disconsolately.

"A well-worn story in our alley."

"Yet it is true."

"Great! And why haven't you popped the question?"

"I can't," he said poignantly.

"Listen, the girl has begged me to tell you!"

He sighed in total despair.

"Go at once and propose to her or let me do it for you," the woman said.

He murmured something incomprehensible as if he were speaking an unknown language. The woman was baffled. He continued his soliloquy: "And God will not forgive me."

"God forbid! Do you think her unworthy of a civil servant like yourself?"

"Don't put words in my mouth, Omm Husni!"

"Speak your mind to me! I'm like a mother to you ..."

"I can't get married ..."

"Let her wait for you for as long as you wish."

"It would be a long wait . . ."

"Give her your word. That would be enough."

"No. I'm not selfish. For the sake of her happiness I must say no."

Before she had time to reply he had left the room. He walked slowly through the narrow lanes. His tribulation was profound and he bitterly accepted that he would not see her again. Yet, despite his anguish, he experienced a kind of relief, desolate and mysterious. If he was relieved, he felt equally certain that he was damned. He loved her, and no one else would fill the void she would leave in his heart. The love he had known would not be easily erased. It would teach him to hate himself and his ambition, but he was determined to cling to it with all the power of loathing and despair. Mad he was, but his was a hallowed madness that slammed the door on happiness with disdain and pride and drove him irresistibly along the path of glory, rough and strewn with thorns. Happiness might lure him into thoughts of suicide, but misery would spur him to pursue life and worship it. But oh, Sayyida, what a loss she was!

TEN

He made progress in every direction, but his torment hardly abated. He was now firmly established at work, and Sa'fan Basyuni, in spite of the failure of his own plans for him, testified to his assiduity, proficiency, and good behavior. He would say of him, "He is the first to arrive and the last to leave, and at prayer time he leads the worshippers in the ministry's prayer hall."

He would often do his own work as well as that of those who fell behind with theirs, and people spoke of his helpfulness no less than of his ability. The tremendous determination with which he advanced in his study promised brilliant success. Obsessively he frequented the National Library, where he read avidly in various fields of knowledge in addition to his difficult study of law. He also became a familiar figure at the Friday prayers at al-Husayn Mosque. He thus became known in the area for his piety and rectitude. Nevertheless his torment was unabated. Sayyida continued to dominate his thoughts.

"She is the one precious thing in my life," he would tell himself.

On the days when they had once had their assignations he would go and sit on the steps of the ancient drinking fountain and suffer the pangs of memory. He would indulge in them until they took form and substance in his mind. In moments of extreme passion he expected to hear her light footsteps and see her approaching, her face aglow with longing and timidity. He yearned for their long talks, their passionate embraces, and each precious spot he had washed with his kisses. But she did not come, nor would she. She had cut him off. Perhaps she had forgotten him, and if his image crossed her mind, would curse him as he well deserved. One afternoon as he was passing under her window, he thought for a moment that he glimpsed her head behind a pitcher placed on the sill to be cooled by the air. But she was not there. Or perhaps she had hurriedly drawn back in disgust. Man was sanctified by suffering, he told himself. Work and worship were inseparable, he told himself again.

One Friday morning he bumped into her in al-Khiyamiyya, in her mother's company. Their eyes met for an instant before she turned them away indifferently. She did not look behind her. He had a revelation of one meaning of death. Like the voluntary exodus of his ancestor from Eden. Like his own lofty struggle with agony.

In his emotional wretchedness he continued to pay cautious visits to the prostitutes' quarter. Time strengthened his relationship with a girl of the same age as he who called herself Qadriyya. Her dark brown complexion, like Sayyida's though darker, attracted him. She was plump but not excessively so. Once their paths had met, quite a long time since, he had never looked elsewhere. Her room reminded him of his. Nevertheless, it was more primitive with its bare floor, its raised bed, its mirror, its solitary chair used both for sitting and for hanging clothes, its washbowl and jug. Because of this he was not able to take off his suit on wintry nights. Years had passed without a

word exchanged between them except for greetings on ar-
rival and departure. Deeply devout though he was, she
taught him to drink the necessary little amount. A glass of
the hellish Salsala wine at half a piastre was sufficient to
blot out his mind and infuse madness into his blood. So
much so that one time he said to her in a moment of
ridiculous ecstasy, "You are the mistress of the universe."

He would contemplate the bare room, smell the incense,
notice the insects, imagine the hidden germs, and ask himself: was this accursed corner burning with the flames of
hell not part of the kingdom of God? On one occasion
there was a thunderstorm and he was incarcerated in the
naked room; the lane was deserted, there was no sound
and darkness reigned. Qadriyya squatted on the bed while
he sat on the bamboo chair. The room was lit by a solitary
candle. As time seemed endless, he took a notebook from
his pocket in which he had written down some notes from
his lectures. He started to read out loud, as was his habit.

"Qur'an?" Qadriyya asked.

He shook his head, smiling.

"Dates with girlfriends?"

"Lectures."

"So you're a student? Then why do you wear a mustache?"

"I'm a government employee. I go to evening classes."

He craved for Sayyida with an aching heart. But an idea
occurred to him which brought him comfort: that the pour-
ing rain was washing the lane and wiping its face clean.

One day he went back to the alley to find the ground in
front of Sayyida's house strewn with sand, while flags flut-
tered on either side. His heart gave a final beat. On the

stairs to his flat he came upon Omm Husni—perhaps she had meant to wait for him? He greeted her as he passed and went on. Her voice called after him, "May God give you what you want and make you happy!"

He could not concentrate on his lecture notes. His small room was invaded by voices, women's cries of joy, children's cheers, and the wedding music. Yes. There was Sayyida entering the kingdom of another man. A period of his youth was over and buried.

He went out with a new determination. He told himself that life was something greater than all its aspirations, that the wisdom of Omar al-Khayyam was more beautiful than al-Ma'arri's* and that a man's heart was his only guide. He stormed into the wedding and the people said he was crazy. He pointed at Sayyida and said to her, "The decision lies with you." She responded to his appeal in spite of the crying and the wailing, because in the critical moments which precede execution the truth is laid bare and death is vanquished. Away they went, running together up three back streets through Bab al-Nasr to the City of the Dead, both staggering with happiness.

The noise, the cries of joy, and the singing continued till dawn broke. He kept looking at his notes without comprehending a thing. He was overcome by loneliness, slumped

---

*Omar al-Khayyam was a twelfth-century Persian poet whose famous *Ruba'iyyat* or quatrains were translated in 1859 by Edward FitzGerald. His verse mocks the transience of human grandeur and calls for the enjoyment of the pleasures of the fleeting moment. Al-Ma'arri was a renowned eleventh-century Arab poet who led a life of celibate solitude and renunciation and whose austerity was reflected in his poetry. *Translator's note*

in an empty world without sound or hope. His anguish bore down upon him on the wearisome path. He reminded himself of the battling of nations and the battling of germs and the battling of health and strength, and he shouted, "Glory be to God on high!"

ELEVEN

His Excellency the Director General

Sir,

I have the honor to advise Your Excellency that as an external student I have, this year, obtained the degree of Bachelor of Laws, seeking to acquire more knowledge and to perfect the tools necessary for a government employee. All along, Your Excellency's genius has been my inspiration under the protection of His Majesty the King, God save him.

Please take note and authorize the enclosed certificate to be kept in my record of service.

I am, sir, with the highest respect,

Your obedient servant

Othman Bayyumi

Archives Clerk

(Incoming Mail)

He had achieved a brilliant record among external candidates. His note addressed to His Excellency would take its splendid course and proclaim to the world his superiority. It would first go to his immediate senior, Sa'fan Basyuni, to authorize its submission to His Honor the Director of Administration, Hamza al-Suwayfi. That meant it would first be recorded in the Archives' register of outgoing mail

and then recorded again in the department's register of
incoming mail. This done, it would be taken to Hamza al-
Suwayfi to approve its submission to His Excellency the
Director General. Thereupon it would be recorded in the
department's register of outgoing mail and then in the register of incoming mail in the Director General's office.
Then His Excellency the Director General would read it.
He would take it in with his eyes, absorb it in his mind,
and maybe it would move him. Then he would sign it and
pass it to the Personnel Office for disposal. Whereupon it
would be recorded in the register of outgoing mail at the
office of the Director General and then in the register of
incoming mail in the Personnel Office. Thus action would
be taken and a copy would be sent to Archives, where the
letter was first issued, for retention in his service record.
In this way the astronomical orbit would be completed and
those who did not know would know.

He was drunk with happiness for a day. But days went
by. What then? Would everything be swallowed up in silence? Nothing happened. The sacred fire burned in his
heart. The shrine of al-Husayn bore witness to his pro-
longed prayers. The path stretched ahead without a single
flicker of light. He had finished his studies but his quest
for culture never ceased. It satisfied his yearning for
knowledge, refining his spiritual qualifications for the position he was one day, by the grace of God, going to fill.
It also fortified him in his long and bitter struggle in the
jungle of officialdom where everyone in power claimed
sacrificial offerings from him. He did not possess the magic
of wealth, nor did he enjoy the privileges which belong to
a great family. No political power was behind him. Nor

was he prepared to play the part of a clown, a servant, or a pimp. He was one of the wretched people who had to arm themselves with every weapon available, seize every chance, rely on God and seek His eternal wisdom which ordained that man should fall on earth in order to rise again, through sweat and blood, to heaven.

With the passage of time in its eternal course a post in grade seven became vacant in the Archives Section when its occupant was transferred to another ministry. Sa'fan Basyuni said to him, "I've recommended you for the vacant post. Nobody in Archives deserves it more than you do."

He shook his hand gratefully and felt he wanted to kiss him.

The old man spoke again: "You've spent seven years in grade eight during which you became a Bachelor of Laws and showed beyond doubt unmatched efficiency." The man laughed, revealing his black teeth with gaps in between, and went on: "It will be yours for sure. People with connections wouldn't be interested in a post at an office inhabited by snakes and insects."

Waiting was long and days went by. Seven years I have spent in one grade, he told himself; at this rate I will need sixty-four years to achieve my ambition. He had not seen the Director General, who had kindled the sacred flame in his heart, since the day he had stood in audience before him among the new appointees. It was his great joy to stand in a corner of the square and watch his procession as he left the ministry with the pomp and circumstance of royalty. That was the goal, the meaning and glory of life.

Work intensified in the department during the preparation of the budget. The Director of Administration needed additional officers from his subordinate sections and Othman was seconded from the Archives. This pleased him and he thought his chance had come. He braced himself for the task with great eagerness. He worked with the auditors and also with the deputy directors. Moreover, he attended meetings with the Director of Administration himself. It was like a volcanic eruption—as if he had just been waiting for the chance ever since his heart had taken fire with sacred ambition. He did not hesitate to place himself at the disposal of his seniors from early morning until midnight. In conditions so critical and delicate the administration was oblivious to everything save true competence. The budget was a serious business connected with the Director General, the Under Secretary of State, the Minister, the Cabinet, the Parliament, and the press. In those busy strenuous days nepotism stood no chance; rather, natural selection prevailed, the competent came to the forefront, and personal ability was recognized, though not, perhaps, rewarded. Othman attracted attention and won full confidence. His extraordinary capacity for work was evident and so was his knowledge of laws and regulations. As if he had not achieved enough success, he volunteered in secret to draft the budget statement which was normally written by the Director of Administration himself. On one occasion he had a chance to see the Director on his own on some business. When he had shown him his papers, he said with great deference, "Director, allow me to present to you some notes I took during work. They may be of some use in the editing of the budget statement."

Hamza al-Suwayfi did not seem to take him seriously.

"You are an excellent young man as everyone says ..." he said kindly.

"I do not deserve the compliment, sir."

"By the way, congratulations! Your promotion to grade seven has been approved today."

This was Othman's moment of triumph. "It's thanks to you and your help," he said gratefully.

"Congratulations!" the Director said, smiling. "But as for the budget statement, that's a different matter."

"Forgive me, sir," said Othman apologetically. "I wouldn't dare to handle the budget statement itself. It's just that I made some notes during work. They're the notes of a hard worker who has studied law and finance and only wished to be of some service to you when you set about composing the real statement."

The man took the notes and started to read them while Othman watched attentively. He found the work absorbing. That was obvious. At last he said with an air of superficial calm, "Your style is good."

"Thank you, sir."

"It seems you are an excellent reader."

"I believe so, sir."

"What do you read?"

"Literature, biographies of great men, English and French."

"Can you do translation?"

"I spend my spare time perusing dictionaries."

Hamza al-Suwayfi laughed and said, "Splendid! Good luck to you!"

He gave him permission to leave and kept the notes. Othman walked out of the room drunk with happiness, convinced that earning the confidence of the Director as he had just done was more valuable than the grade seven itself.

When the draft budget was printed several months later Othman anxiously read the preamble—and there was the passage he had written with his own hand, apart from a slight alteration of absolutely no consequence. He was thrilled, full to the brim with faith in himself and his future. He was wise enough, though, not to divulge the secret to anybody.

It was not long before a decision was made to transfer him from Archives to the Budget Department. That night he stood behind the window in his room and gazed down the alley sunk in darkness. He lifted his eyes to the sky and the wakeful stars. They looked motionless. But there was nothing static in the universe. He thought God had created the beautiful stars to entice us to look upward. The tragedy was that one day they would look down from their height and find no trace of us. There was no meaning to our life on earth save by sweat and blood.

TWELVE

"I'm sorry at your leaving the Archives Section and happy for your sake, in equal degrees," said Sa'fan Basyuni.

In the emotional atmosphere Othman's heart melted with momentary sincerity. Tears came to his eyes as he murmured, "I will never forget you, Mr. Basyuni, and I'll never forget the time I spent in Archives."

"Yet I'm happy because you are."

Othman sighed and said, "Happiness is very short-lived, Mr. Basyuni."

Sa'fan did not understand his remark but Othman lived it. He carried time on his back moment by moment and suffered patience drop by drop. He soon forgot that he was promoted to grade seven or that he worked in the Budget Department. He worked at the ministry like a man possessed, and in his tiny room he delved into more knowledge. Occasionally he would tell himself apprehensively that life flitted by, youth flitted by, and that the river of time flowed on and would not rest . . .

He was still at the beginning of the path. His frugality increased with time and his attachment to his primitive house grew stronger. Money was a safeguard, he felt; and, if need be, it could be a dowry for the bride of his dreams. The bride of his dreams who would open closed doors and entice the treasure of the future out of its hiding place.

Officials had a whole lore of wise sayings and proverbs on the subject. The right bride would be either the reward of glory achieved early or the key to glory that otherwise could hardly be achieved at all. The path seemed long and difficult and he needed succor. Rumor had it that His Excellency the Director General reached his unique position when he was fairly young thanks to politics and family connections and that as a result he married a girl of ineffable beauty from a highly respected family.

It was also rumored that the First Deputy Director of the department was promoted because of his wife, or more correctly his wife's family.

Othman had equipped himself with every possible weapon. Nobody could blame him, then, if he sought the support of a wellborn bride; otherwise how was he to stand against the ruthless current of time? So he started to do translations for newspapers and magazines to earn more money and build up his savings. In this too he was by no means unsuccessful, but he did not spend a single piastre more to alleviate the harshness of his life. Of all the fun in the world he knew only one thing: his weekly visit to Qadriyya in the lane and that hellish glass of wine at half a piastre.

Once she said to him, "You never change this suit. You wear it summer and winter. I've known it for years just as I've known you."

He frowned and said nothing.

"Don't be cross! I like a good laugh."

"Have you counted the money I have given to you over the past years?" he said to her naïvely.

"I once had a crush on a man," she retorted sardonically, "and he stole two hundred pounds from me. Do you know what two hundred pounds means?"

At the thought of such a disaster he prayed to God for protection from the countless afflictions of life.

"And what did you do?" he asked her.

"Nothing. God keeps us in good health. That's what matters."

He told himself there was no doubt that she was mad and that was why she was a whore. But she was the only recreation in his rigorous life and she gave him comfort of sorts. Sometimes he yearned for real love and its charms which gave life a different savor. He would remember Sayyida and the steps of the forlorn fountain and the desert, but in the end he would surrender to the harsh jests of life, resting content with himself, despite the torment in his soul, for having chosen the arduous path attended by the blessing of God and His lofty glory.

One night Qadriyya said to him, "Why don't the two of us go on a picnic on Friday morning?"

He was astonished and said, "I steal my way to you in the dark like a thief . . ."

"What are you afraid of?"

What could he say? She understood nothing. "It wouldn't be right if anyone saw me . . ." he replied in a tone of apology.

"Are you committing a crime?"

"The people . . ."

"You are the bull who carries the earth on its horns . . ." she said satirically.

He was a godly and righteous man with a good reputation to take proper care of.

"You could keep me all to yourself for a whole night," she said seductively. "We could make an arrangement . . ."

"And the cost?" he said warily.

"Fifty piastres."

He contemplated the idea with concern. It would bring him, despite the terrible price, real consolation. And he needed consolation.

"A good idea," he said. "Let it be once a month."

"Would once a month be enough for you?"

"I might come more often, but in the normal way."

He admitted he could not live without her. She was his age, but she appeared insensible to time and the effect it was rapidly making on her. She lived without love and without glory as if, in a kind of fury, she had made a pact with the devil. And how it galled him when she once confessed to him that she had taken part in a demonstration.

"A demonstration!" he shouted angrily.

"What's the matter? Yes. A demonstration . . . Even this back street felt patriotic once . . ."

He told himself that insanity was more widespread than he had reckoned. Political interests exasperated and amazed him. Yet he was determined not to pay attention to them. He believed that man had only one path along which he had to trek without flinching and all alone, taking no part in politics and demonstrations, that only a solitary man could be aware of God and what He wished him to do in this life, and that man's glory was fulfilled in his muddled but conscious effort to distinguish good and evil and in resisting death until the last moment.

THIRTEEN

One day Othman came across an advertisement of some interest. It had been put out by his ministry to fill a vacancy for a translator with a knowledge of both English and French at a salary of thirty-five pounds per month. A date was announced for a competition. He entered the competition without hesitation and without giving it much thought. It so happened that he won it, and this increased his self-confidence and the pride he took in his own talents. He was called to see Hamza al-Suwayfi in his office (the new appointment was under his direct supervision).

"I congratulate you on your success. It shows how versatile you are," he said.

Othman thanked him with his usual politeness.

"But that's a post with a fixed salary," the man said. "If you take it, you will be excluded from the ordinary promotion scale. Have you thought about that?"

He had not in fact realized this and soon his enthusiasm for the job's relatively high salary subsided.

"Actually I do not wish to withdraw from the ordinary scale . . ." he said.

"That means we should appoint the runner-up."

Othman thought of a good idea and said, "Wouldn't it be possible to have me promoted to grade six, add the translation work to my responsibilities, and thus save a considerable sum in the budget?"

The Director of Administration thought for a long while and then said, "The question must be raised with the Personnel Office and the Legal Department."

"Very well, sir."

Hamza laughed and said, "You are ambitious as well as wise. I hope your suggestion will be accepted."

His promotion to grade six was settled at a monthly salary of twenty-five pounds. And though he had to sacrifice ten pounds a month, still he earned a promotion that otherwise he would not have reached for years, quite apart from the special importance attached to him because of his dual job. As usual, he enjoyed a brief spell of happiness. His acquaintance with happiness was ephemeral, like chance encounters on the road. He went back to measuring the long path and groaning at its infinite length. What use was grade six when he was nearing the end of his youth and about to enter a new phase of his life?

Sa'fan Basyuni embraced him and said, "You are making marvelous leaps ahead, my son . . ."

"But days are swifter than a fleeting thought," he said wistfully.

"They are indeed. Heaven protect you from their evil . . ."

Othman gazed at his wrinkled face and said, "Tell me about the ambitions you had when you were young, would you?"

"Me? God be praised! The position of Head of Archives was greater than anything I dreamed of."

"Didn't you aspire to become Director General?"

The old man broke into a fit of laughter until tears came to his eyes. "Common people like us cannot aim at anything beyond being the head of a section," he said.

He was wrong. What he said was true of reaching the position of Minister or Under Secretary of State, but to become a Director General was not impossible for ordinary people. It was their ultimate aspiration, particularly for those special cases who prepared themselves for that exalted glory. But days went by incessantly and stealthily. And the position of Director General would be of no avail if it were not held long enough for it to be enjoyed, for life to be appreciated under it, and for the most sublime of services to be rendered in its name to the sacred apparatus called the government.

When was he going to fulfill the requirements of his faith? Before achieving his life's ambition or after? He must have a family and father children or else he would be damned. Either the bride that exalts a man to glory or the glory that attracts a dazzling bride. Under the intensity of his anguish, he sometimes craved for tranquillity and leisure as he brooded over the hard struggle which gave life its sole meaning and sacred agony.

One day he learned that the Director of Administration, Hamza al-Suwayfi, was complaining that his son was falling behind at school over foreign languages. He offered to help him.

Hamza was undecided and said, "I'd better find him a private tutor. I don't want you to waste your time with him."

"Your Honor," replied Othman in words chosen with his usual care, "you have used words I cannot allow."

So he paid frequent visits to the Director's house and took singular trouble with the boy, with the result that he passed his examination. The Director tried to reward him but he recoiled as though from fire and said, "I shall not permit Your Honor that either ..." And he stood his ground until the man succumbed. Then he added in a grateful tone, "I owe so much to you for your kindness and encouragement ..."

However, he felt in the depths of his heart a pain of similar dimensions to the sum he had magnanimously declined to take. But that was not the only frustration he suffered in frequenting the Director's house. For he had dreamed of coming upon a "suitable" bride there, and who could know? He also dreamed that his services might intercede for him with Hamza al-Suwayfi and enable him to overlook the humbleness of his birth and admit him into a new class that would help him make progress. But the dream did not come true and on his visits the only people he met were males. Sa'fan Basyuni would not have cared about his birth: the origins of the two of them were much the same. But what benefit could he expect from marrying his daughter? Nothing but children and cares and poverty. Not even love. For he only loved Sayyida and his heart had been dead since he abandoned her. But those who aspired to glory on the path to God did not concern themselves with happiness.

Days went by as they always would: the scorching days of summer, the dreamy days of autumn, the cruel days of winter, and the scented days of spring. And he himself would always maintain his patient determination and his soaring ambition, along with the bitterness in his heart and the grinding of his desires.

FOURTEEN

Omm Husni came to see him as was her wont. She presented him with a jar of pickled lemons and sat down on the settee eyeing him carefully and making him curious. She slapped her knee suddenly and said, "By the holy Husayn, your loneliness makes me sad . . ."

He smiled impassively.

"Are you not aware you're growing old?" she said.

"Of course I am, Omm Husni."

"And that nothing is more treacherous than the passing years?"

"You're right."

"Where are your children to keep you company?"

"In the realm of the unknown." He kept quiet for a short while, then said, laughing, "The matchmaker's instinct is stirring in you, Omm Husni . . ."

She laughed and said, "Listen, I've got something special . . ."

In spite of his restraint, the conversation with its engaging air of mystery attracted him.

"You've always got something special."

"A pretty, middle-aged widow," she said hopefully. "A sensible woman. The daughter of the late sheikh of the quarter."

"Eh?"

"She's got one daughter. Fourteen years old."

"They're two women then, not one . . ."

"The girl will live with her uncle. You can be assured of that."

"Great!"

"She is a house owner."

"Really?"

"In Birjwan. It's got a garden with a mulberry tree." She stared at him with her poor eyes to assess the impression her words made. She imagined he was pleased and added, "You'll see her for yourself."

Omm Husni pointed her out to him in al-Sikka al-Jadida. She had a coat on, but he could tell from the slow and swaying way she walked that she had learned it from wearing the long native wrap. She was short and plump with a round face and black hair. She aroused a primitive desire in him. Like Qadriyya. Maybe she was cleaner, he thought, but her troubles were immeasurably greater. He felt sorry for Omm Husni, who knew so little about him despite their long familiarity. How could she grasp what it meant to be an auditor and translator in the Budget Department? Humankind began from clay and was then expected to take up its place among the stars; and that was its tragedy.

"What do you think?" said Omm Husni.

"She's a fine woman," he replied, smiling. "You're still an expert."

"Shall I get on with it?"

"No," he answered calmly.

"Didn't you say she was a fine woman?"

"But she isn't a fit wife for me."

The old woman proved to be more obstinate than he thought, for one afternoon she came to him and said, "What a happy coincidence: Madame Saniyya's come to see me."

His primitive desire was aroused and he yielded to a transient weakness. Omm Husni repeated with fresh emphasis, "She's come to visit me . . ."

"Maybe she will come to visit me too," he said mischievously.

"You could come down if you wished . . ." she said as she was going.

He did go down, without hesitation. As silence prevailed, Omm Husni was able to go on chattering nonstop. Othman remembered that he had never talked to anyone seriously except to Sayyida.

"This is an honor . . ." he was obliged to say.

"Thank you," she mumbled.

"It's cold today."

"Yes."

Omm Husni said to her, "Have you finished redecorating your house?"

She nodded.

Omm Husni also tried to bring him around to talking about his official position but he wouldn't. He was inflamed with desire, but it was desire without hope. Finally Saniyya made as if to go and he got up at once, said goodbye, and left. But instead of going upstairs to his flat he went downstairs and waited below with a daring plan in his mind. He heard her footsteps as she came down the stairs. She was surprised to see him. He feigned surprise as well and said, "Nice meeting you ..."

He made way for her and whispered as she went past him, "Would you care for a cup of tea upstairs?"

"No, thank you," she said hurriedly.

"Please, I've got something to say ..."

"No," she said, protesting.

She went away as fast as she could. He had rushed things, he thought, his limbs trembling with desire. How on earth could he have imagined that she would accept! But what was to be done with sexual desire, impatience, and human frailty? He climbed the stairs, ashamed and infuriated. He would remain an adolescent, he told himself, until he settled down in a respectable family.

FIFTEEN

The state of his purse improved constantly. He received a pay increase and his income from freelance translation was growing. And because he spent only what was absolutely necessary, his balance with the Post Office Savings Bank was steadily going up. His fervor for work never slackened and his relationship with the Director of Administration became close, almost as if they were friends.

One day Hamza said to him, "His Excellency the Director General has expressed his admiration for your style in translation."

A wave of joy overwhelmed him. He became certain he wouldn't be able to sleep a single hour of the night. Naturally, His Excellency did not remember him personally, but he still knew of him, if only as an abstract name. The Director of Administration went on: "His Excellency the Director General is a great translator. He's translated many important books himself, and he certainly knows what he's talking about when he praises your work."

He mumbled gratefully and said, "I only got His Excellency's appreciation through you."

"I've been invited to give a lecture at the Civil Servants Society," the Director said, smiling in a very friendly way.

"I've jotted down the basic points. How about writing it up with your excellent style?"

"It would be a great pleasure, Director," he said in a tone of enthusiasm.

He wished he could be given a similar task every day. For his work in the department, extensive and well appreciated as it was by everybody, was not going to be enough on its own. So the least he should do was to render services to his seniors, and make them feel his importance and outstanding merits. And that might mollify his dismay at the smallness of his achievements when compared with his ambitions. It was something to comfort him as he proceeded on his long path. In the night he was seized with sudden dejection and cried aloud:

"What madness! How could I imagine that one day I would achieve what I desire!"

He counted the grades he needed to pass through before ascending to the pinnacle of glory: grade five, grade four, grade three, grade two, grade one. He counted them and he counted the years they would claim of his life. It made him giddy and a sense of profound sorrow overwhelmed him. Some great event, he said to himself, must take place; his life could not be wasted away in vain. As he had an appointment with Sa'fan Basyuni at the café, he put on his clothes and went out. He found Omm Husni waiting for him on the landing in front of her flat.

"I've got some visitors," she said. "You should come in and say hello. It's Sayyida and her mother ..."

He walked in and greeted them. He was a little frightened at first, but he soon realized that everything was dead and buried. Not a single look of aversion or reproach, but one of unaffected disinterest without a glimmer of recollection. It confirmed for him that the past had fallen into the infinite abyss of death. What added to his profound awareness of the passage of time was the hearty reception the mother gave him. He saw death devouring a loved image which he had believed to be eternal; and all it amounted to was a mere memory that hardly seemed to have once been real, any more than Adam in the Garden of Eden. There was Sayyida, growing fat and stupid. She reminded him of Qadriyya and his agitation grew. The top of her wrap had slipped from her head and rested on her shoulder, leaving both her head and neck free. Her embroidered kerchief was drawn back to disclose a shiny forehead and parted hair. As for the luster he used to gaze at in her eyes, it had gone out. The meeting passed in a lifeless atmosphere tinged with an ironic sense of estrangement. And he tried in vain to trace on those thick lips any sign that his own lips had kissed them. He stayed only as long as courtesy demanded, and when he left, his heart was beating in supplication to the mysterious unknown which wreaked havoc with a smile at once soft and cruel. He was going to meet his old chief, who was going to be pensioned off in a few days, and spend a friendly evening with him. The old man had become skin and bone and lost the last hair on his head, not because of senility, but because of a stomach disease. However he was still as kindhearted and resigned as he had always been. It was obvious that he faced the end of his service in a depressed and melancholy state of mind. Othman tried to cheer him up.

"I wish you a long and happy rest," he said.

"I can't think what life will be like away from Archives," said the old man with a meaningless burst of laughter. "And I haven't got a hobby to keep me busy. That's what really upsets me," he added with a sigh.

"But you're so popular. Everybody loves you."

"True, and I haven't got any family obligations left. But still I'm frightened."

They sipped at their tea while Othman cast furtive glances at him with a feeling of compassion, till the man went on: "I still remember the day I was appointed in the civil service as vividly as yesterday. It is an unforgettable occasion, like one's wedding night. I still remember its every detail. How could a lifetime flit by so swiftly?"

"Yes," murmured Othman with a pang in his heart, "like so many other things . . ."

The man smiled at him as though announcing a change of mood and said, "What about your own family responsibilities?"

He remembered his false claims and replied, "The burden is still heavy."

"You were just a big lad when I first took you on," he said, looking at him with affection. "And now you've become a full-grown man, and soon . . . But anyway, just make sure time does not cheat you. Be very careful."

"Fine! And what good does that do?"

"At least, you mustn't let life pass you by."

"You're speaking of marriage?"

"Of everything. You've always seemed on the lookout to me. But what for? And till when?"

"But life's like that . . ."

The man waved his hand in protest and said, "We all speak confidently about life as if we knew the truth about it."

"What else could we do?"

"Without the existence of God life would be a losing game with no meaning to it."

"It's lucky for us that He exists, and that He knows what He's doing better than we do."

"Thank God for that!" said the old man with feeling.

They fell silent and then talked again, and again they fell silent and again they talked, until it was time to part. Othman felt he was never going to see him again. There was nothing between them but an old comradeship and a sense of duty on his part. Yet he felt for him, momentarily, no little compassion. As they shook hands the old man said, "I trust you won't forget me."

"God forbid!" he answered warmly.

"Forgetfulness is death," said Sa'fan in a pleading tone.

"God give you a long life!"

Othman had no intention of seeing him again, nor had he come to say goodbye to him in response to any genuine feeling, but only for fear of being charged with ingratitude. For this reason he was oppressed by his conscience and his fear of God, and he walked away hardly conscious of his surroundings. In spite of himself, his thoughts were focused on grade five, which was due to be vacant in a few days.

His standing with the Director of Administration was now so good no obstacle of any consequence stood in his way.

So he was promoted to grade five that same month and made Head of Archives.

SIXTEEN

Patience, however vacuous, may have its reward. Othman's new leap forward was a real one and its great advantage lay in the fact that the Head of Archives presented important mail in person to His Excellency the Director General to receive his instructions confidentially and see that they were carried out. God was pleased with him at long last and the celestial gates were now opened to him, leading to the sublime administrative presence. Here was a royal opportunity that required him to exploit all his experience, culture, suavity, and sincerity. Here was the room, vast as a public square, from which he dreamed he would one day rule. It was a dream that had to come true, no matter what offerings must be made at its altar: a dream to which nobody had access save the meritorious who purchased it in exchange for the cheap and ephemeral pleasures of life.

He studied the enormous room meticulously: the smooth white ceiling, the crystal chandelier, the neatly decorated walls, the tiled fireplace, the blue carpet whose dimensions exceeded anything he had ever imagined possible, the conference table with its green felt cover, and the desk facing him with its strong, curved legs and glass top on which stood an array of silver objects: paper holders, inkpots, pens, a clock, a blotter, an ashtray as well as a wooden cigarette box from Khan al-Khalili.

Now he had ample opportunity to cast furtive looks at the lucky Director as he sat on his large chair: sharp dark eyes and a well-shaven face, a dark red tarboosh, a fragrant scent, a black mustache of medium length and width, an aura of vitality all around him, his girth moderate, though his height could not be ascertained with accuracy. Above all an air of solemn and unbending reticence, which made the earning of his friendship an aspiration difficult to achieve.

There he stood in audience before him, conscious of his breathing and within the aura of his fragrant scent, almost hearing his pulsebeat and reading his thoughts. He stood there seeking to learn his wishes and eager to obey his commands before they were uttered. In the light of his smile he read the future; and his dearest dream was always that he would one day sit in his place.

With pious deference he bowed and said, "Good morning, Your Excellency."

The man looked up and mumbled some sort of reply to his greeting.

"Othman Bayyumi, Head of Archives," he announced by way of introducing himself. In the way the Director lifted his normally level eyebrows Othman read the equivalent of a smile, though no smile showed on his lips.

"The new one, sir," he added.

"And the translator. Isn't that so?"

"Yes, Your Excellency," he answered, his heart beating.

"Your style is good," he said in a low voice.

"Your encouragement is a great honor, sir."

"Any important mail?"

He began opening the envelopes dexterously, showing

the Director their contents and scrupulously taking down his instructions. He bowed again and left the room drunk with happiness. On his way back to Archives he thought how Hamza al-Suwayfi was now passing out of his life into the shadows, until the darkness should swallow him as it had swallowed Sa'fan Basyuni, and how from that moment his future was in the hands of (next to Almighty God) His Excellency.

"Beware of slow progress, Othman," he told himself. "One or two leaps forward will be essential."

"When Sa'fan Basyuni was pensioned off he had spent the last half of his service in the same grade," he told himself again.

He knew only too well that the department had two Deputy Directors, which meant that a leap forward could only materialize through Hamza al-Suwayfi: through either his promotion, his retirement, or ... his death. The thought made him feel ashamed, as his thoughts often did, and he prayed to God for forgiveness.

"Why did God create us in such a corrupt image?" he wondered.

He was anything but pleased with that aspect of his own nature, but he accepted it as it was. He believed that on either side of his sacred path the waves of good and evil clashed together, and that nothing could affect its sanctity except weakness, frailty, self-satisfaction, and indulgence in easy delights and daydreams. He prayed: "Forgive me, O almighty God! For my only sin is the love of glory You have instilled in me."

"How can you convince His Excellency of your usefulness? That's the question," he said to himself with determination.

How and when would he have the opportunity to render services without immorality or shame: not as a debtor but as a creditor, in the same way as he treated Hamza al-Suwayfi, and within the limits of dignity and pride, yet according to the dictates of official decorum and its usual obsequious language? "My struggle is noble," he thought to himself. "As for my feelings and thoughts, these belong to God alone."

He believed that God made man for power and glory. Life was power. Survival was power. Perseverance was power. And God's heaven could only be attained through power and struggle.

His chance came when His Excellency Bahjat Noor, the Director General, was awarded the Order of the Nile. He composed a congratulatory column and published it in a newspaper he usually supplied with his translations. He hailed the man's firmness, propriety, good character, administrative talent, and idealism, and declared him a model Egyptian director, a species once thought incapable of replacing the English one.

When he entered the grand room with the mail, His Excellency smiled at him for the first time and said, "Thank you, Mr. Bayyumi."

"Thanks are only due to God, Your Excellency," he said as he bowed.

"Your style is really enviable."

He admitted that it was not only vile wine that made man drunk. But drunkenness did not last and was often followed by a hangover. And he thought the chariot of time was going ever faster. He only remembered that in the distant past, time did not exist: al-Husayni Alley was simply space. Grade five was nothing great for a middle-aged man, a man who constantly lifted up his eyes toward the polestar, who confined himself to his tiny room packed with books, whose best food was ox cheek and kebab on feast days, and whose only pleasures in life were vile wine and the Negress Qadriyya in the bare room.

He needed real human warmth. A bride and a family. He could no longer bear to be consumed in the fire of life on his own.

How he needed a companion in this universe crammed with millions of universes.

SEVENTEEN

He invited Omm Husni to visit him. He made her a cup of coffee on his little stove. She must have felt he was preparing to say something in a mixture of agitation and pleasant anticipation. She said expectantly, "My heart tells me you've called me in for a serious purpose. God be my witness, last night I dreamed . . ."

"Forget about dreams Omm Husni," he broke in. "I want a wife."

Her face beamed with joy and she shouted, "Hurrah! What a happy day!"

"A suitable wife."

"You can pick and choose."

"I've got certain conditions, Omm Husni. Try to understand me!"

"I've got virgin girls, divorcées, and widows both rich and poor."

"Take your mind off our alley and the whole area," he said in a voice of decision.

"What do you mean, my son?" she asked, puzzled.

"I want a wife from a good family."

"What about the daughter of Mr. Hassuna, the owner of the bakery?"

"Forget about our area! A good family, I said!" he interrupted her impatiently.

"You mean . . ."

"Distinguished people ... senior officials ... people in power ..."

The woman was dumbfounded, as if he were talking about the inhabitants of a different planet.

"It seems you're no good in this field."

"You've got strange ideas, my son," she said desperately.

"So?"

"I'm no good, as you said, but I know Omm Zaynab, a matchmaker who lives in al-Hilmiyya."

"Try her, and if she succeeds, I will reward you as if you had done everything."

"You're mean, Mr. Bayyumi," she said laughingly.

"That's unjustly said, woman. I give you my word."

"I'll do my best."

"I don't care if she has been married before. Let her be a widow ... a divorcée ... a spinster. Good looks don't matter as long as she is acceptable; and she doesn't have to be young or wealthy either."

The woman shook her head in bewilderment as he went on: "As for my origins, you can say that my father was a merchant, for example. Do they look into these things to check up?"

"Yes, they do. God bless your parents' souls!"

"Anyway, my person may intercede for me. Just let's try!"

Days went by tiresomely as he waited. And every time he went to Omm Husni, she told him to be patient. His imagination brooded on the reasons for the delay and his spirits were plunged in gloom. He began to frequent the shrine of al-Husayn.

During that period it happened that the Director of Administration, Hamza al-Suwayfi, was confined to bed for some time with high blood pressure. The general situation was critical because the administration was about to start drawing up the new budget. Othman visited the man on his bed of sickness and sat by him for long hours. He showed such sorrow and sympathy that the man sang his praises and prayed that God might protect him against the days of evil. As he sat there, Othman remembered how he had not visited Sa'fan Basyuni and had heard nothing about him as if he had been dead. He said to Hamza al-Suwayfi, "You must rest completely and stay in bed until you're fully recovered. Have no worries about work. My colleagues and I are at your service."

The man thanked him and mumbled anxiously, "The budget draft!"

"It will be done," he answered him confidently. "They're all your pupils and their work under your direction has taught them how to go about it."

At the ministry, there was gossip about the sick man and his illness. It was said that high blood pressure was a grave indication and an incurable disease. It was also said that Mr. al-Suwayfi might have to retire or at least give up his chief responsibilities. Othman listened to these surmises with interest and his heart pounded with secret delight. He deplored and resented this feeling, as usual; but it also roused his dreams and ambitions. Suddenly the Director General set up a special committee, of which he made him president, for the preparation of the draft budget. The implications of his choice were clear to all. True, nobody questioned his competence, or the propriety of the decision from that point of view. But, it was said, would it not have been more appropriate if the Deputy Director of Administration had presided over the committee to satisfy formalities? Nevertheless, he dedicated all his strength to drawing up the draft so that it might emerge perfect and without a single flaw. He demonstrated his skill in the assignment and coordination of duties as well as in gathering the data required from other departments of the ministry. He personally undertook to do the final balance and write up the preamble to the budget. The work required direct contact with His Excellency the Director General in the form of daily meetings which lasted for an hour and sometimes two, until familiarity replaced formality between them. One day the meeting went on for four hours and the man ordered coffee for him and offered him a cigarette, which he refused politely, as he was not a smoker. Days which filled his heart to the brim with happiness, pride, and hope went by. The man was pleased with his work and he felt that God was pleased with him and that fortune smiled on him. He drew up a model preamble to the draft, which the Director particularly liked, and he felt that he was standing on the very pinnacle of glory.

Hamza al-Suwayfi regained his health and returned to work on the last day of the committee's work. Othman showed his delight by embracing him and wishing him long life.

"We were lost without you. The Lord be thanked for your recovery!" he said to him.

"What about the draft?" the man inquired.

"It's been done and the preamble has been written and

both are now with His Excellency for consideration. You will see them tomorrow or the day after. But how are you?"

"I'm all right, thank God. They cupped me and prescribed a strict diet. It's all in God's hands."

"Don't worry. The whole thing is only a passing cloud."

During the course of his long service he got used to his own split personality and the moral conflicts it had to go through. He also got used to disappointments, both those which can be expected and those which cannot—like this one, for example. A feeling of lassitude, almost of despair, oppressed his innermost soul. Thus when a grade four position in the Legal Department became vacant, his anxiety prompted him to speak out. He had never done so before: in the past his habit had been to let his deeds and services speak for him. Thanks to the general atmosphere which his work with His Excellency the Director General created he was able to say to him, "If Your Excellency would be so kind, you might agree to my using my knowledge of the law in the Legal Department."

"No! The Legal Department is a monopoly of people with certain privileges and will be better left alone," the man answered decisively.

Alas, it was the same story as the wife for whom he had been waiting for so long. He was annoyed, but he answered deferentially, "As you wish, Your Excellency!"

He was walking toward the door when he was stopped by the man's voice: "I've proposed in the new budget that the Head of Archives post be raised to grade four."

He turned, took one long step, and bowed until his head nearly touched the edge of the desk.

EIGHTEEN

This was assuredly a gratifying leap forward. If fortune continued to smile on him, he might achieve his ambition in twelve or fifteen years and still have a few years ahead of him in which to exercise high administrative responsibilities like His Excellency. But, as for Omm Zaynab's mission, it was certain she had failed. That could no longer be doubted. A Head of Archives (he thought) was simply not acceptable. A Director of Administration might be accepted, but a Director General would never be rejected, not even if he was a senile dotard.

The reasons for marrying were countless. Marriage was a consolation to the lonely heart and the agonies of solitude. Marriage would also satisfy that religious aspect of his soul which regarded his celibacy as a sin. The tensions in his life were alleviated by the role Qadriyya played in it, but she did not provide him with those feelings of loving kindness, tenderness, and human understanding which marriage offered, not to mention that she intensified his sense of guilt. The only comfort he had was his work, knowledge, and the exercise of thrift. And whenever he was tired of frugality, he told himself, "That's how the Orthodox Caliphs lived!"

One day, as he was working in the Archives, he was taken aback to find Sa'fan Basyuni standing in front of him, decrepit and emaciated like a ghost bidding life farewell. He stood up to welcome the man, ashamed of how grossly he had been neglecting him. He sat Basyuni down, saying with affected geniality, "How nice to see you again!"

The old man pulled himself together with great effort and mumbled, "How I missed you, man!"

"To hell with work!" cried Othman in a burst of repentance. "To hell with home and everyone there! I'm so sorry, dear friend."

"I'm ill, Othman," the man said plaintively.

"Don't worry! You'll be all right ... Shall I order a coffee for you?"

"Nothing at all. Everything is forbidden."

"God give you back your health and strength."

He was extremely vexed and embarrassed and could see no way in which this unfortunate meeting could be brought to an end. Sa'fan was quiet for a short while and then murmured in tones of humiliation, "I'm in bad need of three pounds." He choked as he spoke and then went on: "For treatment, you see."

Othman trembled. He saw danger about to engulf him, no mercy shown; and he cried out passionately, like a man being chased, "How horrible! I would never have ... I would never have imagined myself turning down a request from you. Particularly this request. I'd sooner steal than say no to you ..."

The man swallowed hard and said despondently, "Not even one pound?"

"Don't you believe me, dearest of men? Oh, God! If only I could tell you! If only I ..."

The man despaired completely and was lost in unknown thoughts. He got to his feet with difficulty, saying, "I believe you. God help you! God help us all!"

Othman's eyes brimmed with tears as he shook hands with him—genuine, unaffected tears, condensed out of the vapors rising from the tortuous conflict raging deep down inside him. He nearly went after him, but let him go and walked back to his desk muttering to himself, "Oh, God!"

"We should have been hewn out of stone or iron to be able to stand up to life," he said to himself.

"The path is very long," he also said. "My only consolation is that I hold life, the gift of God, as sacred and do not make light of it."

During the same week he heard the news of Sa'fan Basyuni's death. It was not unexpected, but he was deeply shocked. From the sheer intensity of his pain, he screamed inwardly, "Stop suffering! You've got more than your share of pain."

And he said, "People envy me, but am I happy?"

And he asked, "What's happiness?"

"Our real happiness," he told himself, "is that God exists," and he then added with determination, "Either we live or we die!"

NINETEEN

Time cuts like a sword. If you don't kill it, it kills you. He had become an authority on getting the better of time, but had he really escaped its sharp edge? The previous day a new young employee had spoken to him privately, asking his advice on a personal matter.

"I really feel embarrassed about this, sir," the young man had begun, "but I come to you as a father or an elder brother!"

The words sounded so strange he thought the man was being sarcastic. As a father! True, he could have had a son of his age. And why not? Yet he never failed to attend to techniques of mastering time.

One day Omm Husni said to him, "This time it's a headmistress."

He shook with unconcealed pleasure. But although a headmistress could perhaps make a suitable wife, yet what he really desired was someone to lift him to a higher plane. So what was to be done?

Unable to resist his curiosity, he asked the old woman, "Old?"

"In the prime of womanhood. Thirty-five years at most."

"A widow or divorced?"

"A virgin, as God made her. Headmistresses were not allowed to marry in the old days, as you know."

He did not think he would be any the worse for seeing her, and see her he did, in al-Sayyida. He liked her appearance and she had a good figure. (His instincts had been aroused by Saniyya before.) So he saw her and learned that she too had seen him.

Later on Omm Husni said to him, "She won't cost you a penny."

He realized the woman had approved of him. For here she was, offering to furnish a house and provide the wedding requirements. All he would have to attend to were minor matters.

The old woman went on: "Only the ring and a wedding present and some sundries. So, can I congratulate you?"

"Let's be patient a little!"

"Her only condition is the promise of a hundred and fifty pounds in case of divorce."

Everything was fine and in perfect harmony with his cautious nature. Had he wished only to satisfy his religious faith by getting married, nothing would have been more suitable. But what about his worldly ambitions? He sank in a whirlpool of thoughts, perhaps because of his feeling that he was growing old. Because of the secret revelations which enveloped him from the world of the unknown. Because of the irony and cruelty and treachery of appearances. Because of the roses he never smelled and the songs echoing beyond the range of his hearing. Because of life's harshness and deprivations. In spite of all this he said to himself, "What's all this brooding and hesitation for? Rubbish! All is rubbish! I will not do something crazy after all that waiting."

He wished he could establish a relationship with her: an

unholy relationship! But he was only likely to be rejected, even more flatly than he had been by Saniyya. Even if she agreed, it would not be an occasion for happiness, as one might think, for that would require him to rent and furnish a flat somewhere else. His heart was full of apprehensions and in the end he simply said to Omm Husni, "No."

"You can't be serious!" the old woman shouted.

"I said no."

"You're a riddle, my boy."

He laughed mirthlessly.

"What do you want? Do you not like the female sex?"

He laughed again.

"God forgive you!"

"I'm sad, my son," she said.

"In sadness," he said to himself, "man is hallowed and made ready for divine joy."

TWENTY

Onsiyya Ramadan arrived at a time when Othman had fallen victim to feelings of melancholy and depression which he had not experienced with such force before. He told himself that he was lost in an arid and blazing desert, that he had gained nothing of value, that ambition needed time, and life was short and the past despicable. For all his intimate personal emotions, he was despicable. His true emblem was a charity grave and the prison. The one martyr in his family had died on the side of oppression and injustice. He was friendless. Relations between him and the companions of his boyhood had ceased altogether. At work he had colleagues who respected and envied him but he had no friends. The only man with whom he could sit and talk was a servant at al-Husayn Mosque, and the only touch of romance in his arid life was a bare room and a whore who was half Negro. "What's the meaning of this life?"

True, he had dedicated himself to the glorious path of God, but he was wading in sin and suffering pollution hour by hour. And it seemed he did not resist death with sufficient fortitude. "It looks like a losing game!"

As he burned in the furnace of his mental hell, a soft breeze with a new fragrance was wafted into Archives. It was new not only to Archives but to the whole administration, and new in the full sense of the word. It was the first girl to join the administration and, specifically, the Archives Section. A handsome dark-skinned girl of delicate features and simple dress. Her appearance as she stood in front of his desk to introduce herself left him at once confused and astonished and moved. As he asked her to sit down, he glimpsed the clerks' heads beginning to protrude from between the lines of filing cabinets. They were amazed and unable to believe what they saw.

"Welcome!"

"Thank you! My name is Onsiyya Ramadan."

"Pleased to make your acquaintance! You seem to be very young?"

"No, I'm eighteen!"

"Wonderful ... wonderful! And what qualifications do you have?"

"The General Certificate of Education in science."

"Splendid! Why didn't you carry on with your studies?" He regretted that question, remembering the first day of his service at the office of His Excellency the Director General.

The girl answered shyly, "Certain circumstances compelled me to stop."

He cursed circumstances and sought relief in the fact that the two of them shared the same dreadful predicament.

"You reminded me of myself. But let me tell you this: I got my degree while working. Closed doors will open before those who try hard," he said affably.

Her eyes clouded over with a wistful look and she said, "But we live in a harsh and unfair society."

He found that the "revolutionary" ideas which he had

no knowledge of and deliberately sought to ignore were threatening again to assault him. He said with determination, "It's better to rely on oneself than to attack society. God addresses His commandments to us as individuals and brings us to account also as individuals. And to cleave a path through rocky ground is better than begging charity from society. It seems you're interested in politics and what they call sociological thinking?"

"I believe in it."

"This means you don't believe in yourself. As for me, I only believe in my own willpower and the unknown wisdom of God!"

She smiled and did not utter a word. He smiled too and said, "I will give you the incoming mail to look after. It's the best job for a new employee."

"Thank you, sir."

"I will expect you to prove yourself always worthy of my confidence."

"I hope I'll never give you reason to be disappointed."

"If you meet with any annoyance from your colleagues, do not hesitate to tell me!"

"I hope I won't need to."

He handed her over to one of the clerks to initiate her in her job.

"Incoming mail," he said tersely.

He felt that Archives had made a gratifying leap toward the luminous life and that from now on it would not lack something to move the heart and excite the senses. The clouds of melancholy memories lifted a little, and instead his thoughts turned back to Sayyida, to Saniyya, to Asila the headmistress, and to Qadriyya, and he told himself that the world of women was endlessly variable and sweet and painful. He asked himself in puzzlement, "Which is the means and which the end: the woman or the position?"

And he also said to himself, "Many men live without position, but who lives without a woman?"

At his age a man thinks twice. He gets tired of the company of books and grumbles about work. He finds deprivation and austerity difficult to bear and is conscious of the past pursuing him without mercy. At his age a man's awareness of his isolation and estrangement grows more intense. So does the anxiety of waiting for uncertain glory. The previous day Hamza al-Suwayfi had said to him, laughing, "Look! There's a gray hair on your head, master of financial statutes!"

He started as if he was caught red-handed.

"Your eyes may have deceived you, sir."

"Let the mirror be the judge between us. Have a good look at home."

"It's come too early," he muttered in defeat.

"Or too late!" the Director of Administration said, laughing. "I knew gray hair when I was ten years younger than you."

He gave another long laugh and then went on: "Yesterday you were the subject of a conversation I had with some colleagues. We wondered how you lived. They said no one ever met you on the street or saw you at a café or a party, and they wondered where you spent your time. 'What does he live for without a family?' they said. And 'He's not interested in any of the things that interest most people; what does he really care for in this life?' "

Othman smiled weakly and said, "I'm sorry to have been a source of trouble to you."

"You're an able and honorable man, but you're mysterious. What is it you care about in this world?"

His heart raced as the questioning closed in upon him, and he said, "There's no mystery, Mr. Suwayfi. I'm a man whose interest is in carrying out his duty and who finds his heart's content in worshipping God."

"Well said! I hope I haven't upset you. To be at peace with oneself is what really matters."

But where was this kind of peace? Where?

Here was gray hair advancing on him. Life's splendors, like its trivialities, drew to an end. How much time was left for him?

TWENTY-ONE

One day while Othman was doing some routine work with Hamza al-Suwayfi, the latter remarked in the course of a conversation, "Happiness is man's goal in life."

"If that were so," Othman replied with concealed contempt, "God wouldn't have banished our first ancestor from Paradise."

"So what do you think the purpose of life *is?*"

"The sacred path," he answered proudly.

"And what's the sacred path?"

"It's the path of glory. Or the realization of the divine on earth."

"Do you really aspire to dominate the world?" Hamza asked in surprise.

"Not exactly that. But there's an element of divinity in every situation."

The man gave him a strange look which made him regret his words. "He thinks I'm mad," he said to himself.

A rumor spread around that His Excellency Bahjat Noor was going to be transferred to another ministry. When he heard this, his heart nearly jumped out of his breast. He had done the impossible to gain the great man's confidence. How long would it take him to gain that of his unknown successor? But the rumor proved false. One day Bahjat Noor handed him a huge bundle of papers as he said, "This is a translation of a book on Khedive Isma'il. It took me half a year to do it!"

Othman looked at the papers with interest.

"I'd like you to look over the style," the man continued. "Your style really has no equal."

He received the commission with total happiness and addressed himself to it zealously, energetically, and with meticulous care. Within one month he had returned the manuscript to His Excellency in perfect style, thus rendering the sort of service he had always yearned for. His Excellency was now his debtor, and at every meeting he was now greeted with a smile that even the most favored were not honored with.

Despite all this, his soul was still scourged by apprehension. He saw time running past him until it disappeared into the horizon, leaving him behind, all alone in the wilderness clasping his sacred ambition. His anxiety drove him to visit a woman who read fortunes from coffee cups, half Egyptian, half European, in al-Tawfiqiyya. She stared into the cup while he watched her, half excited and half ashamed. He told himself he should not have given in to superstition.

"Your health is below par," she said to him. His physical health was good beyond question. But his mental health was not. Perhaps she was right after all . . .

"You will get plenty of money but only by dint of much trouble," the woman went on.

He was not after money, albeit he held on tight to every piastre he earned. Perhaps she meant salary increases that would come with promotions ordained in the world of the unknown.

"An enemy of yours will go on a journey from which he will not return."

Enemies were legion. They hid behind charming smiles and sugarcoated speeches. In his way there was a Deputy Director in the third grade, another in the second, and a Director of Administration in the first. They were all friends and enemies at the same time, as life with its pure intentions and its cruel demands dictated.

"I see two marriages in your life."

He had not even succeeded in finding one, but such was the punishment of those whose misgivings led them into superstition. On his way home he remembered Onsiyya Ramadan. She was growing healthier in appearance and better-looking: a good job was quick to show itself on the faces of the poor. He was a kind chief to her. A tender and decent human relationship, as yet difficult to name, bound them together. At any rate, he no longer was able to imagine Archives without the fragrance of her presence there.

When he had returned to his room, Omm Husni came up to him and said with an air of concern which made him smile, "Madame Asila is at my place. She . . ."

"The headmistress?"

"Yes. She wants to ask your help with some of her affairs."

He realized at once that she had come to snare him with her charms. His natural expectancy drove him toward adventure. He shook hands with Asila for the first time. She was wearing a blue dress which did justice to her breasts and forearms and emphasized the attractions of her figure. There she was, offering herself to him, no matter what true or false stories she had to tell. She excited him as Saniyya and Qadriyya had done. They were of the same type: voluptuous and exciting but not fit for marriage.

Omm Husni said, "I'll go and make you coffee."

Always the same tactics! And old woman whose sole concern was to see people lawfully wedded. Here they were, sitting on the same sofa with nothing between them but a cushion. He tilted his head to straighten his mustache, meanwhile casting a glance at her well-rounded leg firmly planted in a masculine-style low-heeled shoe.

"I'm honored, madame!"

"The honor is mine."

She clasped her hands in her lap and said with a firmness which displayed her ability to face up to the situation, "May I ask you a question?"

"Madame?"

"I own a piece of land which has been expropriated by the government. I'm sure you understand these matters?"

"Of course."

"The road they're going to build covers most of it but leaves bits which cannot be put to any use."

"I believe this is taken into consideration when the valuation is made."

"But the procedures are complicated, as you know."

"You may depend on me."

By the same measure as he sensed the strength of her personality he despaired of seducing her. She was prepared to marry him and in fact she came for nothing else. But for her to acquiesce to an illicit relationship with him looked impossible. Omm Husni came back and they started to drink coffee in total silence. Perhaps she was the most suitable wife on several counts, but she was not the one he wanted. Out of the blue came the image of Onsiyya Ramadan placing itself between them and effacing the woman completely. Since the days at the ancient fountain, his heart had not moved as it did for that young girl. His strained nerves relaxed and his mind was set at ease as he received from his imagination a fresh breeze reawakening his noblest feelings. When the woman had gone, he found Omm Husni looking at him anxiously for reassurance on the success of her purpose in life, on which she spared no effort and which had become part of her faith. The old woman had come to worship marriage and children and the festivities associated with them, and she praised God for the miracle of love which He had created. When his silence continued, she said hopefully, "Maybe you've changed your mind?"

"Why should I?"

"Didn't you see how beautiful she is?"

He remained silent, adamant in his rejection of the hand she stretched out to him in kindness.

In a voice of disappointment Omm Husni began: "As the proverb says . . ."

He left the room before he could hear the proverb. What a pity! Unless a valuable marriage came to his rescue, his pains were likely to be wasted and his hopes destroyed in midcourse. His life had become the object of endless questions and criticisms. People wondered why he didn't marry and have children and make friends. They also wondered how he could live entirely in his private world and ignore the national events taking place around him which excited people even to the point of giving up their lives. And what were the causes which preoccupied them and possessed their hearts, hovering above the noise of their conversations and hindering their work? They talked endlessly about children, diseases, food, the system of government, class conflict, political parties; they repeated proverbs and clever sayings and they cracked jokes. They did not live a true life: they ran away from their sacred duty. They recoiled from taking part in the fearful race against time and glory and death, and in the fulfillment of God's word, which was withheld from the unworthy.

TWENTY-TWO

Onsiyya Ramadan came to submit her monthly report on the incoming mail. It was the morning of an autumn day and the cool weather breathed into the recesses of the spirit a feeling of sweet wistfulness. His eyes turned now to the paper he was examining, now to her fingers spread out on the edge of the desk. He thought he saw something move in one of her hands. Something which moved and came nearer, delicately inching its way as if bearing a secret message. It was a small package, which she neatly slipped under the blotter after making sure he had seen it.

"What's this?" he asked in a low voice which instinctively responded to the air of caution evident in her gesture from the start. He lifted the blotter a little to reveal a silver-colored case half the size of an open palm.

"What's this?" he asked again.

"A small present," she whispered, blushing.

"A present?" he asked, though he did remember.

"It's your birthday!"

A surge of ecstatic joy overwhelmed him. Today was indeed his birthday or, to be precise, coincided with the date of his birth. But it was just another day. He might remember it a few days before it came or a few days after it had passed or even on the actual day, but this never made any difference except perhaps in that it served to intensify his apprehension of the future. He never celebrated the occasion. That tradition was unknown to him and to the alley he had been brought up in. But here was Onsiyya announcing new traditions. New too was her innocent maneuver to show affection and her marvelous power of opening up the gates of mercy.

"As a matter of fact, I never bother to remember it."

"That's strange!"

"But you shouldn't have taken the trouble!"

"It's only a very simple thing."

"I really don't know how to thank you."

"There's nothing to thank me for."

"What a lovely person you are! But how did you know the date of my birth?" he asked, then laughed and went on: "Ah! I forgot that ... You've dug out my service file and now you know my age!"

"It's the age of reason and maturity."

He put out his hand and shook hers. He pressed her hand, smooth as silk, and all this time sweet thoughts poured over him. He would buy her an even better present on *her* birthday, which he would learn from her service file too. In spite of his radiant happiness he wished she could have chosen a way to express her feelings which had nothing to do with money; for the spending of money hurt him and upset the balance of his life. But he did not dwell on this for long. He was slipping into an abyss, flying toward the unknown, his heart filled with delight and longing. When he pressed her hand, she accepted it with a conscious smile, which gave him encouragement as well as pleasure.

And after this, what? Was this in harmony with his one and only path? He was confronting something greater than a delicate and transient moment perfumed with enchantments. He was confronting the unknown: Destiny itself. He was knocking on a door behind which time was stopped in its tracks or even made to go backward. "Come back," a call resounded, "or thou perishest!" But no ear listened, no heart responded.

On the following day she stood in front of him transmitting looks full of submissiveness and sweetness. His head was on fire, his throat scorched. His fingers were drawn toward hers and touched them where they rested on the files spread out between them. He looked warily around, while he mumbled some meaningless instructions. He bent forward and kissed her lips, then sat back again in his chair, shivering, burning, intoxicated with life and the fear of the unknown.

TWENTY-THREE

They met early one Friday afternoon. Their assignation grew out of an irresistible urge to surrender, coupled with a hope that he would be able to escape in the end. He felt it a fall from grace but it was steeped in happiness. He had no knowledge of places where lovers met. She suggested al-Azbakiyya Garden. He objected on the grounds that it was unprotected and open to view from all directions. But the Zoo was sufficiently far away and deserted, lying outside the built-up area and safe from the eyes of busybodies. To reach it the tram had to pass through open fields and wastelands. They walked side by side enjoying a "real" life in the few hours before closing time. He had not been to the Zoo since visiting it on a school outing. He had no idea what was customary when taking a girl out: what may be said and what may not, what may be done and what may not. They walked together happily and quietly; yet there was that uneasy feeling nagging at him and telling him that the meeting was something irregular and wrong, that he should not have given way to the impulse. To ward off his feelings of confusion and frustration he expressed his admiration of the trees, the bridges, the grotto, the streams, the ponds, and the different kinds of animals. But he remained convinced that he had not yet said a single word to the point and that he was trying to escape when it was already too late. She walked beside him, her eyes melting with a dreamy and triumphant look, her head raised and her breast thrown proudly forward. Her air suggested to him a tide race of demands within. And in her breathing he felt that she took in the most beautiful mysteries of life. Their eyes met, and in her glowing look he read the purest innocence, sweet cunning too, and the rush of secret desires.

"Even now that I've got a job I can't easily get out of the house," she protested.

"Don't let it make you cross, my dear," he answered in a ludicrously paternal tone.

"But it's unnatural and humiliating."

"An inaccurate translation of the parental sentiments."

"I don't think you really believe that."

"Really?"

She laughed with complete assurance and added: "If my mother had known I was coming to see you, I don't think she would've minded."

"But she didn't know?" he said anxiously.

She laughed again and was silent for a moment until his mouth went completely dry. Then she said, "Our meeting remains a secret as agreed."

"Of course, dear."

"To tell you the truth, I'm not happy about this."

It was obvious she wanted everything out in the open, and what that meant was also obvious. Was he then at her mercy already? Would circumstances compel him to accept things that were not in his plan? Would the powers of destruction besiege him and shatter for good his solitary, sacred, unattainable dream? Through his fearful thoughts he challenged the unknown and threatened it with murder.

But then he felt ashamed of his thoughts as he noticed the gazellelike figure prancing merrily along beside him, her arm in his, while the clouds moving through the sky above the gardens seemed to give a benison to her joy. He soon calmed down and buried his misgivings. He made peace with his importunate ambitions so that he might melt away into the glow of enchantment and swallow down the taste of hellfire burning inside him. He felt his elbow touch her supple body and receive from its youthful and untrodden territories vibrations of magic. He looked carefully around with a stealthy and guilty look, then kissed her cheek and her neck. Their lips met. He said in a voice which he did not recognize, "You're adorable, Onsiyya."

She smiled coyly and happily.

"I wish," he murmured passionately, "I wish I could . . ." and then he fell silent, breathing audibly.

"Yes?" she said.

"It's as if I'd known you since eternity."

She smiled contentedly, though her eyes asked for more.

"How beautiful the place is!" he said. "Everything is so unspeakably beautiful."

"You love nature!"

Her remark struck him as strange and ironic, seeing that the reality of his life was so different.

"It's you who have made everything beautiful."

"Don't exaggerate! Would you mind if I told you something?"

"Not at all!"

"You don't seem to be interested in anything."

"Really? And do you believe that?"

"I don't know. But I feel you're a man of riddles just as I feel you're a good man."

"All this is nonsense! There's only one universally acknowledged truth: that you're charming."

"And so?"

"What's between us must remain forever, whatever happens in the future."

"In the future?"

"Didn't you learn something unpleasant from my service file?"

"Nothing at all."

"You're the most beautiful thing in my life."

"And you too," she said in a quiet voice of surrender.

He kissed her cheek again as he passionately squeezed her hand.

"I'm torn between what I want and what I am able to do."

"Is there something that you wish for and cannot do?"

"Life is full of unattainable wishes."

"Tell me about what concerns *me*!"

She was right. His mouth was still moist from kissing her and his elbow still touched her soft sweet body as they paced in front of the elephant which saluted them by lifting its trunk.

"Let our relationship remain a secret!"

"Why?"

"So that nobody may think badly of us."

"And why should anybody do so?"

"People would."

"There's nothing bad between us."

"But that's what people are like, my dear."

She laughed lightheartedly and asked, "Did you ask me to go out with you, sir, in order to preach to me?"

"I asked you because I wanted us to get to know each other and because I wanted to make sure my heart was right."

"And what did you find out?"

"I have become certain that the heart is the best guide!"

All the way back he was wondering why he had not revealed his love to her in direct terms. Why did he not ask her hand? Even supposing she would turn his life upside down and make him face a new direction at the altar of life, was she not more capable of making him happy than the polestar?

TWENTY-FOUR

Asila Hijazi, the headmistress, came again on the pretext of asking whether his good offices had succeeded—or so Omm Husni told him when she invited him to come down to her flat. He was staggering under the weight of his usual cares in addition to the new love which intensified the conflict inside his mind to the point of madness. Thus he welcomed the visit of Asila Hijazi in the hope of escaping from himself. Even if that meant committing a folly that would cost him nothing. He needed a way out and Qadriyya was not available every day. He shook hands with the headmistress and sat down, saying, "Your problem is moving toward a solution."

Soon her physical charms, emphasized by her flower-spotted dress, began to chant their infernal song. She looked at him affably and asked, "Will I have to wait long?"

Omm Husni thought she would go and make the coffee and he was seized with an insane determination to settle the matter there and then and strike an unexpected blow regardless of consequences.

"No, you won't have to wait for long."

"I'm really grateful."

"In fact, everything depends on the strength of your nerves."

"It seems I will have to wait for some time?"

"Allow me to express my admiration!" He said this in a completely different tone as if to introduce an entirely new subject. She blushed and lowered her eyes.

"I really admire you," he went on, "as a man admires a woman. You understand what I mean."

She did not utter a word, but she looked happy as though she were about to be admitted to Paradise.

"But we must be careful. I must tell you something else which I know you might not like."

She gave him an inquiring glance.

"The idea of marriage is out of the question!" He watched her as she turned into ashes, then added boldly and ruthlessly, "I've got a thousand and one reasons, and life, you know, is full of secrets."

"What makes you tell me that?" she asked weakly.

"It's not as though we were two adolescents," he answered politely, but persisting in his cruelty. "Let's talk like adults and look for happiness with sincerity and courage."

"I don't see what you mean."

"Well, I admire you, but I am a bachelor forever."

"Why do you tell me that?"

"I thought you might have a solution for my incurable case."

"You insult me inhumanly," she said with great indignation.

"Forgive me! I speak out of a deep sense of agony."

She frowned and kept quiet.

"A little courage could give us considerable happiness."

"How do you mean?"

"Isn't my meaning clear enough?"

"I don't think I understand you."

"We need a safe place to meet at," he said, with a presumption he never thought he could muster.

"Mr. Bayyumi!" she shouted.

"It'll be a real consolation for two people in need of love and intimacy," he went on heedlessly.

She stood up in a fury, saying, "Either you go or I go."

"I'm going, but think about it calmly and objectively. And don't forget I'm a poor man!"

TWENTY-FIVE

It was no longer a question of a single silver hair difficult to spot. Every now and again a new one would peep out with a chilling white look which threatened a change in the rhythm of life. And what was life? A passing game that a man played with reluctance until he found himself face to face with his ultimate fate. Then he would survey his life in its entirety, weigh his deeds and assess their fruits, suffer however resentfully the breath of the unknown, brace himself for further struggle, and then accept defeat. But at least let that defeat be hallowed in the event. There was no promotion to look forward to in the near future. His savings increased, his nervous tension grew more acute, his efforts redoubled. His relationship with Onsiyya was growing more and more intimate, slowly but surely. As for Qadriyya, she truly deserved to be described as a lifetime companion. At the end of his prayers he would say to God, "What's life, O God, without You?"

But apparently others did not have his staying power. For his telephone rang one day and the caller was none other than Asila Hijazi, the headmistress.

"I wanted to thank you for your successful mediation."

"Don't mention it, madame."

"And how are you?"

"I'm fine, thank you."

"I'm glad to hear it."

"Thank you."

"I'm really grateful for your help."

"You're very kind."

A few seconds of silence and then: "But I have a bone to pick with you."

"God forbid!"

"Last time when I left you I was angry, don't you remember?"

"I'm sorry, but there was nothing to make you angry."

"You think so?"

"Yes."

"But you didn't try to get in touch with me."

"I'm sorry, but I don't know your phone number."

"But I managed to get yours!"

"I'm sorry again."

"I hoped you'd try to make the situation easier with a kind word."

"I'm more than willing."

"Really?"

"Positive."

"How?"

"Let's agree on that!"

"Are you still poor?" she asked, muffling a laugh.

"There's no helping that."

"We're lucky I've got enough money."

"May God give you more!"

"Should I be more explicit?"

"I'm more than willing!"

"Lovely! Let us each do our part then!"

This was no surrender, it was a breakdown. He could imagine what lay behind it. She was in her middle years, approaching her decline, lonely and trembling at the advance of age. No youth, no real beauty. Certainly there had been a conflict in her mind which he had not perceived, but he was now witnessing its distressing consequences. What was he to do? He was frightened of Onsiyya and had no real desire for Asila. In his moments of despair he often wished that his heart could die and his lust could be quelled, so that he could go forward carefree on his arduous journey. And to himself he said sorrowfully, "I can't blame people who think I'm mad."

TWENTY-SIX

How would he find the time to look for a flat and furnish it? He let days go by without doing anything. He forgot the matter altogether until one day he found Asila standing in front of his desk. He received her with a smile, though silently cursing her.

"Excuse my boldness . . ." she said.

He smiled without comment.

"I couldn't get any sense out of you on the telephone."

"I'm much too busy these days," he said with a solemnity to match the official surroundings.

"What have you done?"

"Nothing."

"Nothing at all?"

"Work doesn't give me a free minute. Believe me!"

"I expected to find you more eager." She spoke with a boldness which sounded like desperation; like one whose patience was ebbing as his fears increased.

"I am eager enough, but I have no time."

"There's a flat in Rawd al-Faraj . . ." She held out a folded piece of paper as she went on: "Here's the address. Go and have a look at it yourself. And if you like it, go ahead and have it furnished." Then temptingly and beseechingly: "I hope you'll like it. Who knows, it may bring us happiness."

He felt the crackle of approaching fire. When the

woman had gone, he thought of the long nights that would be added to *The Thousand and One Nights* rather than of the nights he was accustomed to spend studying, translating, and performing services for His Excellency: nights of sacrifice on the path of glory. That path which he had chosen from the first day as an emblem to which his infinite yearnings could legitimately aspire. His desire for the woman subsided as a result of her thoughtless impetuosity and the way she had freely offered herself. Actually she was not bad as a substitute for Qadriyya. But in her he felt the crackle of approaching fire, eager to swallow him up together with those sacred hopes linked to the mystery of God's word. He would not let himself be destroyed by any power on earth save death itself—which was another of God's mysteries, like His inspiring glory. And while he had not been accepted by that unknown wife after whom he had striven for so long, it would be wrong to give up the struggle and surrender to pathetic widows and spinsters.

One night he heard a knock on his door. He was dumbfounded to see Asila sneak in, stumbling over her shame and humiliation.

"I was determined to come and told myself that if somebody saw me I would make for Omm Husni's flat as if it had been her I had come to visit." She spoke in tones of embarrassment as she sat down panting on the settee.

"Well done!" he said, trying to comfort her.

"Do you mind my coming?"

Life had begun to stir in his depths.

"Of course not. I'm more pleased than you imagine."

"Omm Husni will soon be going to bed," she went on. "Do you mind if she suspects what's happened?"

"Not at all!"

They exchanged a long look. Beneath its darkly flowing current she seemed without a trace of pride, merely a woman in love with her defenses down.

"What've you done?" she asked in tender expectation.

He recovered completely from his surprise. He did not want to talk about anything at all; all he was aware of was carnal desire embodied in a woman prepared to give herself to him. He took her soft hand. It felt cold; the contraction of her heart had stopped her blood from circulating. He squeezed it repeatedly, as if passing a secret message. She wasn't expecting this—or so she pretended —and tried to take her hand away. But he did not let her.

"What've you done?"

"We'll discuss that later."

"But you haven't tried to get in touch with me." He bent toward her and kissed her cheek as he whispered in her ear, "Later . . . later . . ."

"But this is what I've come for."

"You'll get what you're after . . . but later . . ."

She opened her mouth to speak but he stopped her with a long and heavy kiss, saying sharply, "Later."

Nature played one of her infinite tunes with joyful bravura, which seemed like a miracle. But soon the tune died away, receding into oblivion and leaving behind a suspicious silence and a feeling of languor full of sadness. He lay on his side on the bed while she stayed where she was on the settee, exposing her slip and the drops of sweat on her forehead and neck to the unshaded light of the electric bulb. He looked at nothing and wished for nothing, as if he had accomplished what was required of him on earth. When his eyes turned in her direction, they denied her completely, as though she had been some strange object sprung from the womb of night, and not that enchanting person who had set him on fire: a dumb thing with no history and no future. He said to himself that the game of desire and revulsion was no more than an exercise in death and resurrection, an advance perception of the inevitable tragedy, matching in its grandeur such fleeting revelations of the unknown, in its infinite variety, as are granted. The position of Director General was one such revelation, but it could only emerge in response to a soaring effort of the will, not to its capitulation, however attractive. Thank God he was barricaded behind sensible impassivity, lethal though it was. Here was this woman, eager beyond question to return to her important subject but hesitant and ashamed. She must have hoped that he would make the first move; but despairing of this, she cast him a wistful beseeching glance and mumbled, "So?"

The unfamiliarity of her voice astounded him with its intrusion on his sacred solitude. He felt a steady repulsion toward her which nearly turned into hatred. What she was seeking to do was to pull down the edifice which he had been constructing stone by stone.

"What do you think?" she asked.

"Nothing!"

The roughness of temper characteristic of the back streets, and latent in him, was discernible in his voice.

"But surely you must've done something!"

"Nothing at all."

"Haven't you even had a look at the flat?"

"No."

Her face darkened with chagrin.

"Forgive me for saying this, but ... should I put the money in your hands?"

"No!"

"Frankly, I don't understand you."

"I've spoken clearly."

"What do you mean? Don't torture me! Please."

"I don't intend to do anything."

"I thought you had agreed and promised," she said in a trembling voice.

"I don't intend to do anything."

"If you have no time now ..."

"I have no time now, nor will I in the future."

Asila breathed heavily and said with a break in her voice, "I thought you felt differently."

"There's no good in me," he confessed. "That is the fact of the matter."

She shied away as if she had been stabbed. She put on her dress in a hurry, but she collapsed again onto the settee, overcome by fatigue. She rested her head in the palm of her hand and closed her eyes; he thought she would faint. His heart beat violently, rousing him from his impassive cruelty. If the unthinkable happened, he might well face a scandal with profound repercussions. The path was rough and arduous enough in spite of his good reputation. What would happen if he suddenly found himself involved in a scandal of the kind the newspapers like to gloat over? He nearly changed his whole attitude and risked a new lie, but at the last moment she moved. She got up with some difficulty, made her way, subdued and crestfallen, to the door and disappeared from his view. He sighed deeply with relief, then stood up and walked to the window. He looked out at the alley, nearly covered in darkness, until he saw her pass, swiftly and ghostlike, out the front door. She went on through the alley toward the end leading to al-Jamaliyya and soon vanished completely into the dark.

Nobody, he told himself, knew the unknown, and for that reason it was impossible to pass comprehensive judgment on any of our actions. Yet for man to define a goal for himself provided him with a guide in the darkness and a justification in the clash of fortunes and events. It was also an example of the design Nature seemed to adopt in her infinite progression.

TWENTY-SEVEN

He loved Onsiyya Ramadan. He had to confess that before his own conscience and before God. Since the time of the ancient drinking fountain his heart had not sung so sweet a song. And for this reason he should be more afraid of her than of any other woman on earth. What made it even worse was that she too loved him; yet a wife who could not push you forward would only pull you back. He might perhaps have married her without hesitation if there had been only one step between him and the Director General's position. But things being what they were, what would he gain from marriage save the daily troubles and cares which consumed a man's energy in ways it had not been created for?

One day Mr. Husayn Jamil brought him the mail as usual. When he had put his signature to it with his instructions, the man did not leave as he normally did. He was a young Archives employee who had worked under Othman for five successive years and who was known for his perseverance and good manners.

"Is something the matter, Husayn?"

The young man was quite clearly confused. There was something he wanted to say. What could it be?

"What's wrong? Is it something to do with your work?"

The youth came closer as though to make sure his voice was not heard by others.

"I'm afraid something is the matter, sir," he said.

"What is it, my son?"

"I'm awfully sorry, but I must speak up."

"Well, I'm listening."

He was quiet for a moment while he pulled himself together.

"It's something to do with Miss Onsiyya Ramadan."

Later on Othman told himself that he probably had not heard the name uttered or that he had heard it without comprehending what it meant.

"Huh?" he said, stupefied.

"Onsiyya Ramadan!"

"Your colleague? What about her?"

"The truth is," came the almost inaudible answer, "I'm in love with her."

Othman frowned and his heart missed a beat.

"And what has that to do with me?" he asked angrily.

"I wanted to propose to her."

"Fine! But what have I got to do with it?"

The youth looked down and mumbled, "But Your Excellency . . ."

Othman's limbs were trembling. The questioning stare he gave the young man was tantamount to surrender.

"Yes?"

"Your Excellency knows everything."

"How do you mean, please?"

"The truth is, if it hadn't been for you, I would have proposed to her."

Othman was certain it was all up with him. Nothing was any longer of value. Not even life itself.

"If it hadn't been for me?"

"I've seen everything . . . here and outside," came the despondent reply.

With the strength of despair, Othman prepared to defend himself to the end. He was not so much sorry for his lost love as he was afraid for his official position.

"Young man, you have a nasty mind. What is it you've seen, you wretch? But of course, this is just what lovers do! I've always treated her as if she were my own daughter: a totally innocent relationship. I'm very much afraid you have damaged her good name without knowing what you were doing."

"I know when and how to bury my sorrows and protect the reputation of someone I love." There was a certain nobility in the young man's innocent and grave rejoinder.

"Good . . . good . . ." sighed Othman. A wave of sorrow swept over him. "You've behaved like a man." The force of the initial shock and the relief brought by his unexpected escape were so jarring that he felt sick. "A man like you deserves to be happy with the person he loves."

His tormentor left him and he remained alone with his sorrow, a sorrow as solid and as gigantic as fate itself. It brought back to him old memories of long, sad nights. He thought to himself that if life was measured by its share of happiness, it was certain that his own had been a sheer waste. Why did the pursuit of glory demand such suffering?

TWENTY-EIGHT

He asked Onsiyya to meet him in the desert by the Pyramids on a Friday morning. This time he planned the assignation with more caution than was his custom, stealthily giving her a piece of paper on which he had scribbled the arrangements and the route each of them should separately take. It was one of those wintry mornings, dry and cold, though both of them felt the sun's rays warm and invigorating. He watched her all the time with genuine anguish, though he was conscious that the role he was playing was cruel and debasing. From the first, the girl seemed unusually anxious.

"I had such a strange feeling when I read your note," she said. "My heart just shriveled up inside me."

Woman, he thought to himself, possessed an instinct which guided her in the knowledge of her most intimate affairs without recourse to the intellect; and if humanity as a whole had this sort of instinctive access to the unknown, it would not have remained unknown.

"The truth is," he said with increasing sadness, "we've got to think about this thing."

"Which thing do you mean?"

"Our close and sacred relationship."

"What's wrong with it?"

"You must have wondered at my silence. We've talked about everything except the most essential, and naturally you may never have realized that all the time I've been suffering the torments of hell."

She touched his arm concernedly.

"I must admit you're making my heart shrink even more!"

"And I must admit that I'm a selfish man."

"No. You are not selfish at all," she protested.

"Yes. Selfish in the full meaning of the word. And because of my selfishness I've led you on and given you false hopes. I shall never forgive myself."

"You've been so kind and good to me."

"Don't try to acquit me. You must have often wondered, 'When is that man going to speak? What does he want of me? How long shall we go on meeting and parting without really getting any further? Is he toying with me?' "

"I've never thought ill of you."

"In fact I have asked myself these questions many times, but the illusion of happiness has always got the better of me, and I wasn't able to face up to reality before things got out of hand. How often have I been determined to tell you the truth, but then weakened and given in!"

"What truth?" she asked in a tone of frustration.

"Er . . . Why I haven't proposed to you . . ."

Her eyelids quivered when she heard the beloved word. She stared at him in alarm and then turned away, raising her eyes to the unknown as though in silent prayer to ward off disaster.

"Surely you must have asked yourself this question? Otherwise what's the meaning of life?"

She fixed her gaze on the ground as though, expecting only the worst, she no longer wanted to know more.

"I'm ill," he went on.

"No!" she exclaimed in genuine fear.

"I'm not fit for marriage."

She stared at him, stunned.

"Don't let my appearance deceive you . . . My illness is not fatal, but it makes it impossible for me to marry."

He looked down in distress. The sharp sigh he heard transfixed his heart. He was on the point of casting off the shackles of his ambition, throwing himself down and kissing her feet and begging her to accept him as husband. But another force held him back and paralyzed him.

"I've spared no effort. I've been to more than one doctor. I never lost hope, or else I would have told you a long time ago. But it's no use. I should put an end to my selfishness, otherwise I will have destroyed your future forever."

"But how could I live without you?"

"You're still young. The wounds of youth are quick to heal."

"I can't believe it. It must be a nightmare."

"It wouldn't be wise for us to carry on together any longer."

"I can't believe it."

"Sudden disasters are always hard to believe, but life sometimes seems a series of sudden disasters. What matters is that you should find your way before it's too late."

"What do you want to do?" Her voice broke with anguish.

"We should stop traveling up a dead end."

"I can't."

"It's got to be done. It would be sheer madness to continue."

He avoided her eyes. He had carried out his plan successfully to the end. But success was harsh, and he now found himself alone in a wilderness of desolation, alone with his anguish and shame, without faith, without solace. Madness was the only way out, he told himself. Madness alone had room for both belief and disbelief, glory and shame, love and deceit, truthfulness and lies. For how could sanity stand the absurdity of life? How could he look up at the stars when he was sunk up to the neck in slime? Through the long night he wept and wept.

TWENTY-NINE

It seemed that a gleam of light sought to pierce the dark clouds. He learned that Onsiyya Ramadan had become engaged to Husayn Jamil. He delighted in this happy development which made him feel secure at last, and he said to himself, "Now I can mourn for my lost love with my mind at rest and no apprehensions to bother me. I can drink out of the well of anguish until it runs dry and I gain my freedom. And in this I'm an expert."

Throughout his life he had met no woman more fitted than her to make him happy. Not even Sayyida. She was beautiful, intelligent, and pure and she had truly loved him. He now had come to believe that he was never going to find anyone like her again, no matter how lucky he was; and that, after all, was a just punishment.

The tide of time brought about another event. Hamza al-Suwayfi, the Head of Administration, was absent from work one day and it was learned that his blood pressure had risen to an even more critical level than that of his first attack. Othman went to visit him. This time he found him prostrate and completely resigned, the shadow of the other world looming in his clouded eyes. His appearance moved Othman greatly and he saw in it the final scene which awaits all men, whatever their position.

"You'll be all right, my dear fellow," he said. The sick

man smiled, feeling grateful in his utter helplessness for any kind word.

"Thank you. You are a good man, just as you're a capable and efficient one."

"This is only a passing cloud. You'll soon be back running the administration."

The man's face contracted as he tried to hold back a tear.

"I won't be going back."

"Oh, come on!"

"It is the truth, Mr. Bayyumi."

"You always exaggerate."

"It's what the doctor says. He told me frankly that if I did exactly what I was told I could survive this attack, but that I had to retire from my work at once."

Othman's feelings were mixed, but for the moment compassion was dominant.

"Put your trust in God's mercy," he said. "His miracles are endless."

"Work isn't important to me anymore. I've married off my daughters and my youngest son is now in his final year at the School of Agriculture. I've fulfilled my calling and all I need now is peace of mind."

"May God grant your wish!"

Despite his exhaustion, the sick man went on with an air of pride: "God be praised. I've done my duty toward my job and toward my family. I've never been in need and I've always had many good friends. What more could one hope for?"

"A man of your fine character deserves all that and much more."

"We pass away one after another. Do you remember the late Sa'fan Basyuni? Men go, but their good deeds remain forever."

"True, true!"

The sick man stared at him for a long while and then said, "May God guide you to where your happiness lies."

Othman was much moved at the time and for a long while after. The moral of the situation pierced his heart as if he was returning from the burial of a close friend. But he roused himself in the nick of time and said to himself, "The sorrows of this world exist to sharpen our determination, not to dull it."

His thoughts were riveted on the position which would soon be declared vacant. He was by general agreement an able, honest, and upright man. In fact, nobody doubted that he was even more efficient than the two Deputy Directors of Administration. But one of them was in grade two and the other in grade three. If justice was done and efficiency alone was the yardstick, he would become Director of Administration; but how could he jump straight from grade four to grade one?

Hamza al-Suwayfi was pensioned off at his own request and consequently a flurry of promotions took place throughout the administration from grade one down to grade eight. So Isma'il Fayiq became Director while Othman Bayyumi moved up the scale to grade three and became Deputy Director. Thus an attack of high blood pressure had given a nudge to the wheel of fortune, bringing good luck to some and ill luck to others.

Othman was happy with his promotion for a day or two

but his happiness soon wore thin. Hamza al-Suwayfi had been an able official, but now that he had gone, nobody was better qualified to replace him that Othman; and it was really grotesque that a man like Isma'il Fayiq should become Director of Administration.

Othman went to His Excellency the Director General's office to thank him. He had no doubt that of all the employees he was the one the Director General liked and valued most, relying on him in the official work of the administration as well as in his own private activities. They shook hands and Othman expressed his gratitude with his usual eloquence.

His Excellency said, "You didn't know the full story. I had on my desk a pile of recommendations from the Minister, the Under Secretary, and many members of Parliament . . ." The great man stared at him for a while before going on.

"I told them, 'You can have anything you want, except that *one* promotion must go to someone whose only recommendation is his ability and character."

Words of gratitude poured from Othman's lips; the frustration he felt in his heart he did not mention. The Director General continued: "We both know that Isma'il Fayiq is weak and ignorant."

"Yes, of course, Your Excellency," he replied, annoyed at the mention of the man.

"This means that actual responsibility will be yours alone to shoulder even though you are only Second Deputy."

"I shall always be at your service."

"What could I have done?" Bahjat Noor went on apologetically. "He is a relative of the Under Secretary, as you know."

"It's not your fault, Your Excellency."

"Anyway, congratulations again. And rest assured you are going to get your full rights one day."

He left the room satisfied in some degree, but his irritation soon got the upper hand and the joys of promotion were forgotten. He cursed everybody without exception and said to himself in terror that life went faster than any kind of promotion.

Before he left the Archives Section, his staff came to congratulate him on his promotion and say goodbye to him. When it was Onsiyya's turn to shake hands with him, he noticed, in a welter of confused emotions, the swelling of her belly with its promise of happiness. Already a wife and expectant mother! No doubt her husband, Husayn, would be particularly glad about his transfer to the administration.

He took his seat as Second Deputy Director, but he felt superior to all those around him. He stood first in the Director General's confidence, being an authority on administrative matters, regulations, and the budget, not to mention his mastery of law and economics, his general knowledge, and his erudition in languages. But he asked himself, "What's the use of all these advantages when life flies by or a sudden illness descends?"

He knew that both the First Deputy and the Director of Administration were younger than he. Consequently their positions were unlikely to become vacant unless an unpre-

dictable miracle, a sudden death or a road accident, occurred.

"Forgive me, O God, for my wicked thoughts!" he
prayed. Each of them (he kept thinking) enjoyed good
health, a carefree nature, as well as a closed mind. And
nothing, nothing save the lofty position he longed for
could make up for the tremendous sacrifices he had made
at the expense of his life's happiness and peace of mind.
Perhaps he had never felt at any time in the past as he did
now the need for the sort of wife who would help him up
the ladder before he reached retirement age or fell sick or
died. So he asked Omm Husni to speak again to Omm
Zaynab, the marriage broker, about him, now that God had
raised him to grade three as Deputy Director.

He was extra careful nowadays when he visited Qadriyya in the prostitutes' quarter, and he decided to disguise
himself as a member of the lower classes so that nobody
would recognize him. So one night he went to her wearing
a loose galabiya, a cloak, and a scarf. She did not recognize
him until she heard his voice.

"Been sacked from the government?" she asked, almost
beside herself with laughter.

She had been slowly going downhill, growing all the
time more fleshy and more debauched. Yet the relationship
between them had grown stronger and developed into real
human intimacy. It had passed through all the natural
phases of desire, boredom, and then indispensable habit.
Thus she and the bare room and the horrible wine had
together become something integral and familiar, which
simultaneously gave him comfort and sorrow as well as

something to think about. It also impelled him to face up to life, harsh and primitive as it was. He took no notice of the woman's indifference or of her despicable behavior. In fact, these very elements made it possible for him to enjoy, even while he was with her, his sacred solitude.

"Strange," he would say to himself, "that in all my years I haven't made love to an ordinary woman except once!" He remembered Asila, but he also remembered that what he had done with her was a criminal act and not an act of love.

And he would also say to himself, "There is a humane and wholesome way of making love."

Then he would sigh and say, "But there is glory too."

Then he would sigh more deeply and say, "There is God as well and He is the origin of everything."

Then he would sigh more deeply still and add, "And we remember Him when times are good and also when they are bad!"

THIRTY

Despite her resistance to the passage of time, age had left its imprint on Omm Husni. Her eyesight was almost gone and she limped so badly that she could only walk by supporting herself with an old broom handle. Meanwhile Othman had so completely despaired of Omm Zaynab, the marriage broker, that he told himself indignantly that those who chattered about class conflict had good reason to!

Omm Husni was no longer fit for her noble profession. Her senility was such that once she suggested a woman for him forgetting that she had died years before.

One afternoon, after Friday prayers at the mosque, he was sitting in the Egyptian Club coffeehouse when he saw Asila passing, accompanied by another woman. He recognized her at once, though the extent to which she had changed was dreadful. She was as flaccid as a punctured ball, and in her face the springs of femininity had dried up, leaving behind an ambiguous shadow that was neither feminine nor masculine. She walked clumsily, a model of misery and degeneration. Something told him that death was hunting her down and that it also was drawing closer to his own time and place; that his time which had once seemed hallowed in eternity was no longer secure behind the screen of sweet illusions and that the proud and everlasting truth was now revealing itself to him in all its awesome cruelty. Did Asila still remember him? She could not have forgotten him. He had penetrated into her very depths with the full weight of his deceit and egoism, leaving her thereafter to hate him and curse him.

As for the companions of his boyhood, they were petty by profession and all they did was father children and fill the air with meaningless laughter. And gone were the innocent passions and the unruly imagination of childhood, buried under thick layers of dust like al-Husayni Alley, which had changed its skin. Many old houses had been demolished and small blocks had taken their place. A small mosque now occupied what used to be the donkey park and a lot of people had left the quarter and gone to al-Madhbah. Everything was changing: electricity and water had been introduced into houses, radios blared night and day, and women were abandoning their traditional wrap. Even good and evil had changed and new values arisen.

All this took place while he was still in grade three and growing old. Was this the reward for his extraordinary effort and dedication? Did they not recognize him as the epitome of expertise based on both theory and practice? That if his official memoranda, his budget analyses, and his original pronouncements on matters of administration and on the purchase and storage of goods were collected in book form, they would constitute an encyclopedia of government affairs? For such a shining light to be hidden away in the position of a Second Deputy Director of Administration was like hanging a 500-watt electric bulb on the wall of a toilet in a tiny village mosque.

He also told himself that "government official" was still a vague concept inadequately understood. In the history of

Egypt, an official occupation was a sacred occupation like religion, and the Egyptian official was the oldest in the history of civilization. The ideal citizen of other nations might be a warrior, a politician, a merchant, a craftsman, or a sailor, but in Egypt it was a government official. And the earliest moral instructions recorded in history were the exhortations of a retiring official to his son, a rising one. Even the Pharaohs themselves, he thought, were but officials appointed by the gods of heaven to rule the Nile Valley by means of religious rituals and administrative, economic, and organizational regulations. Ours was a valley of good-natured peasants who bowed their heads in humility to the good earth but whose heads were raised with pride if they joined the government apparatus. Then would they look upward to the ascending ladder of grades which reached right to the doorstep of the gods in heaven. To be an official was to serve the people: the competent man's right, the conscientious man's duty, the pride of the human soul—and the prayer of God, the creator of competence, conscience, and pride.

One day he went for an inspection tour of the Archives Section. There he saw Onsiyya, whose womanhood had now reached the stage of maturity. She had also moved up the official scale to become a supervisor, occupying the post which was made empty by her husband's transfer to the Ministry of Education.

"A long time!" he could not prevent himself from saying as he shook her hand.

She smiled in unaffected shyness.

"Are you happy?" he asked.

"I'm all right."

"The ability to forget is one of fortune's blessings," he said, yielding to an irresistible impulse.

"Nothing is forgotten and nothing remains," she said with friendly simplicity.

He thought about her words for a long time, and as he left Archives, he repeated to himself, "I loved you so much, Onsiyya, in the old days."

He returned to his office to find on his desk a circular from the Public Relations Section. He could tell from its appearance that it was the kind which announced the death of an employee or the relative of one. The circular read: "Mr Isma'il Fayiq, the Head of Administration, died this morning. The funeral will take place . . ."

He read it a second time. He read the name over and over again. Impossible. Only yesterday he had been working in full health. Othman had had his morning coffee with him in his office. Indeed the man had said, giving voice to his familiar worries, "The country is awash with contradictory opinions," at which Othman had smiled without comment.

"Everyone," Isma'il had gone on, "believes he's been sent by Providence." Then he had shaken his head and said, "In what frame of mind can one begin to prepare the final accounts?"

"In one like mine," replied Othman in an undertone of sarcasm.

The man had given a loud laugh. He had never questioned the efficiency of his deputy or the fact that he was the backbone of the administration. How *could* the man have died, in heaven's name?

Othman went to the First Deputy, who had been an intimate friend of the Director.

"Do you know anything about this tragedy?"

"He had just started on his breakfast," the First Deputy replied in a stunned voice, "when he suddenly felt tired. He got up and went to lie on the couch. When his wife came up to him to see what was wrong, she found him already dead!"

One felt relatively secure, thought Othman, because one believed that death was logical, that it operated on the basis of premise and conclusion. But death often came upon us without warning, like an earthquake. Isma'il Fayiq had enjoyed perfect health until the last moment, and what happened to him could happen to anyone. Wasn't that so? Health then was no guarantee, nor was experience, nor knowledge. Fear shook him to the depths. "The best definition of life is that it's nothing . . ." Othman said to himself.

But was death something so unfamiliar? Certainly not, but seeing was not like hearing, and his fright would surely persist for a day or two. For in moments like this, profit and loss and joy and sorrow canceled each other out, and things lost their meaning.

"What's the value of a lifetime of dedicated work?" he would ask himself.

His misgivings stayed with him during the funeral. Even the chitchat of the employees did not deflect his thoughts from their wistful course. But he felt grateful to be alive. "What is true heroism? It is to go on working with undiminished zeal in spite of all that."

His preoccupation with the post of Director of Administration soon drove all other thoughts from his head. The First Deputy had been nominated for a job in the judiciary system. This left the way clear for himself. He would be promoted to grade two and appointed Head of Administration. After a year's work in the post he would be eligible for substantive appointment in the post. Hope was now something he could really and truly grasp.

But he was totally dismayed by the decision to appoint someone from the Ministry of Transport as the new Director of Administration.

THIRTY-ONE

No ... No ... No ...

This possibility had never crossed his mind. He hated His Excellency Bahjat Noor and cursed him a thousand times. Bahjat Noor should have stood up for him. Damn them all! Did they think he could work for the benefit of others all his life? And who was this new Director? Who was this Abdullah Wajdi? How could he introduce himself to him as one of his staff? The shame of it! Shame would pursue him down the corridors of the ministry, and many were they who would gloat over his plight!

Bajhat Noor called him to his office.

"I'm very sorry, Mr. Bayyumi."

"I've come to despair of doing my best in life," he answered, not seeking to conceal his indignation.

"No, no. He is a relative of the Minister."

"I have learned to envy lazy officials."

"I repeat, I'm sorry, and I can tell you His Excellency the Under Secretary is sorry too." The Director General was silent for a moment and then went on: "Don't despair! It's been agreed to promote you to First Deputy this month as soon as the present one has left."

No use. Promotions did not matter except as a means to his most cherished hope, the hope to which he had dedicated his life. The new Director was a young man of only forty, which meant that, if things went their natural course, he would be pensioned off as a Deputy Director or at best, and then only by a miracle, as Director of Administration. The dream of his life was shattered and the past was dead and buried, leaving behind it only the blackness of illusion. Perhaps he would have been better off driving a cart like his father. For the first time in his life despair overcame him and he felt the end of his life much closer than the achievement of his precious hope.

A new idea possessed him with a force he had not experienced before: marriage. He should not procrastinate any longer; procrastination would serve no purpose. It was enough that the best time of life for love and marriage was gone. How he yearned for a wife, for genuine affection, for an honest partnership, a warm house, children, a human relationship, a loving heart, a kind touch, conversation, a refuge from torment, a shield against death, a savior from loss, a prayer niche worthy of true faith, a resting place secure from foolish dreams, a truce with frugality and deprivation and loneliness.

"Woman is life, and in her presence Truth is crowned by Death itself with all Death's solemnity."

He would not resort to Omm Zaynab, nor was there now anything to be gained from Omm Husni, crippled as she was. But there was a new girl in the administration called Ihsan Ibrahim to whom he had unhesitatingly expressed his affection. For now he did not want to delay his marriage for a single day if he could help it, and each extra night he slept alone made him all the more frightened. It was as though the desire for marriage had constantly smoldered inside him until it finally erupted like a volcano.

But Ihsan did not take his affectionate hints in the right

RESPECTED SIR

way. She probably thought it inappropriate for a man of his age to court her. But what could he do, since he was no longer capable of the kind of love he had experienced in the days of Sayyida and Onsiyya, or the wild passion he knew in the days of Saniyya and Asila.

One day Ihsan happened to be in his office on some business or other. He seized the chance and said to her, "Do you mind, Miss Ibrahim, if I ask you a question which may sound a bit curious?"

"Of course not, sir."

"Are you engaged?" he inquired after some hesitation. She blushed and for the first time glanced at him with the eye of a female rather than an employee working under him.

"Yes, sir."

He was disappointed.

"Forgive me, but I hadn't noticed a ring on your finger."

"I meant, I'm almost engaged."

After a moment's reflection he said, "May I ask you something ... something that must remain a secret between us?"

"Sir?"

"Could you help me find a wife?"

She was confused for a while and then said, choosing her words, "All my friends and relatives are about my age. They wouldn't suit you, I'm afraid."

A polite way of saying, "You wouldn't suit them," he thought.

"Is it impossible for a man of my age to get married?" he asked, his desperation nearly driving him beyond the limits of propriety.

"Why not? There's a suitable wife for every sort of age."

"Thank you, and please forgive me for bothering you!"

"I hope I may be of some service to you."

When she left, he was burning with anger. She should have accepted him for herself, he thought, or for one of her friends or relatives. He had become unwanted scrap then, like the rubbishy surplus from the ministry's Supply Section, which he put up for sale every year after the annual stocktaking. Evidently his lot in the marriage stakes was to be no better than that. Not even if he achieved his most cherished hope and the dream of his life, by occupying the office of His Excellency the Director General. The whip of time continued to lash his back, and he could run no longer. And with each day that passed he became more and more obsessed with the idea of marriage till it bulked as large as his obsession with promotion. Ihsan brought him back no answer. Madly he began to make advances to women in the streets and on buses but he had no experience in that sort of thing and had to give it up. "What a waste my life has been," he would often sigh to himself.

Indignantly he asked himself what it was which so stood in the way of his getting married even after he had relinquished his early cumbersome conditions. Age was no doubt a negative factor, but it was not everything. People probably inquired about him and knew all there was to know about his origins. That was the other shameful fact. The truth was, he was a man past his prime and also of lowly background. God knew what else they said about him; for an outstanding personality like himself would naturally arouse envy in the hearts of others. He had long felt that he was without a true friend in this world; that he stood aloof, high above human frailty.

Night took him as usual to Qadriyya and the bare room.

"How nice," he would say to himself with bitterness, "to have a Deputy Director's job and a whore who is half Negress as my lot in life!"

"This is the first time you have drunk a second glass of wine!" she said laughingly. "It must be the end of the world!"

The end of the world it was, for he felt a strange giddiness in the head.

"Qadriyya, you must know I'm a man of faith," he said apropos of nothing in particular.

"Thank goodness!" she said as she tied a red kerchief around her coarse hair.

"And if I didn't believe that the world is sanctified by being the creation of God," he went on, "I would be content to live like an animal."

She gazed at him stupidly and said, "They've decided to abolish us, damn them!"

"And God in His greatness ..." he continued, disregarding what she said.

"They've decided to abolish us," she interrupted.

"I beg your pardon?"

"Haven't you heard the news about the abolition of prostitution?"

No, he hadn't. All he read in the papers were obituaries and affairs of state.

"Really?" he asked with alarm.

"They've actually told us so."

"Unbelievable!"

"They've promised to help us find work. Work indeed! God damn them in this world and the next! Have they reformed everything till they've only got us left to worry about?"

"Maybe it's only a rumor. This country is full of rumors, you know."

"I'm telling you, we've been officially informed."

"And when is this going to take effect?" he asked in real consternation.

"Before the end of the year."

They were quiet, and for some time the noise of revelers in the lane could be heard in the room. He had imagined many disasters but this one never crossed his mind.

"There'll be brothels everywhere," he observed wistfully.

"And VD will spread."

"Thousands of innocent girls will be corrupted."

"Those wretched idiots! Just for the want of something to do!"

"What are you going to do?" he asked her with a sigh.

"Whatever happens, I am not going to work as a washerwoman in a hospital."

"Could I have your home address?"

"We'll be watched."

"Haven't you thought about the future?" he asked, his despair becoming unbearable.

"I will get married," was her confident reply. "There's nothing else for me to do."

Her words fell on him like a blow. He poured himself a third glass.

"Anybody in particular?"

"It won't be difficult to find somebody."

"But how?"

"I've got five hundred pounds," she replied boastfully. "I could furnish a flat for a hundred and fifty and keep the rest as something to fall back on. That being so, wouldn't lots of men be keen to marry me?"

"I'm sure you're right."

"If you find a suitable husband for me, let me know," she added, laughing.

At midnight, as he stealthily found his way under the arches, he bumped into a drunken man being sick. He was nauseated beyond endurance. A sense of his loneliness, of despair, and of the emptiness of life overtook him: he felt an urge to do away with himself. He changed his direction without thinking and staggered his way back to the lane. He saw Qadriyya coming down the stairs on her way home. He stopped her with his hand and said, "Qadriyya, I've found a suitable husband for you." He did not see her face in the dark but was able to guess the impact of his words.

"Let's get married at once!"

THIRTY-TWO

The marriage took place on the following day. His decision did not stun the woman as he had expected. She just looked at him closely for a while to make sure that he was serious, then she nodded her head with approval. He told himself that she probably considered him the real beneficiary in the deal because of her five hundred pounds.

"Let's go to the Registrar's Office at once!" he said with a sense of urgency.

"Sober up first and wait till morning," she said, laughing happily.

He spent the night in her little flat in al-Shamashirji Close and in the morning he said to her, "Let's furnish a new flat and then get married."

"No, we get married first and then furnish a flat," she retorted in tones of determination and finality.

The Marriage Registrar was called to the house. The contract required two witnesses and she could only find two pimps who used to procure men for her. He watched in a stupor during the simple ceremony. What was happening? A feeling of anxiety, almost of terror, took hold of him and tore him apart and he prayed that the unknown might intervene to rescue him from this nightmare. This feeling then gave way to one of resignation, almost of recklessness.

When he stated his name and occupation to the Registrar, both the woman and the pimps were amazed. He told himself they would declare him crazy, as others had done. Certainly he himself might as well admit, from now on, that he was out of his mind. A woman who was half Negress, gross as a fat cow, and laden with half a century of lechery and dissolute living. So the crazy longing he had sought to satisfy had come true: he had become a husband and Qadriyya, the companion of his youth, had become his wife. What had he done to himself?

"I must begin a new life . . ." he said.

Because he had come to like the Rawd al-Faraj quarter since he used to visit Hamza al-Suwayfi, he rented a flat there consisting of three rooms and a lounge and they set about furnishing it together. He forced her to wear the veil, ostensibly in the name of modesty, but his real motive was to guard against her being recognized by one of her old customers. They bought furniture for a bedroom, a dining room, a living room, and a study. They also bought new clothes for both of them, a radio, and a few other things. They contributed a hundred pounds each toward the cost, for with the same spirit of recklessness he had changed his policy and spent money freely wherever the need arose with a sense of desperate resignation which blacked out the pain he usually felt in such circumstances. A strong desire possessed him to enjoy the pleasures of life of which he had always deprived himself.

He said goodbye to Omm Husni in a touching scene. The old woman was taken aback at his decision to move.

She wept and said to him, "Don't run away from the place you were born! It's not good."

But run away from it he did, and without regret. In any case he couldn't conceivably bring Qadriyya to live in al-Husayni Alley. He generally thought of the place as a symbol of decay, of privation, of a wasted life, and of sad memories. He sought to drown his visible as well as his secret sorrows in what pleasures were available. And he determined to remind himself, or rather convince himself, that Qadriyya was the only woman he had really loved. Or else how could he have kept up his relationship with her for a lifetime? As for her, she spared no effort in playing her part as a housewife in her new and "fashionable" surroundings which represented a fantastic leap from the old lane. He prayed to God that none of her old customers would ever set eyes on her and advised her not to mix with the neighbors.

"Why not?"

"I don't like their manners."

But what he really feared was that she might have a disagreement with one of her neighbors and that this would put an end to her reserve and cause the volcano of obscenities latent in her to erupt. Otherwise, he could not deny that she was making a real effort to make him happy and to adapt to her new situation, and as time went by he grew more confident about his new life and accepted it for what it was. He enjoyed the company and the comfort, the discipline and the cleanliness that it afforded him. And now he was able to perform his prayers with a clean conscience. He even felt that having saved a soul that had gone astray (perhaps two souls rather than just one), he was closer to God than ever before.

Thus he bought a plot in al-Khafir Cemetery, after consulting people who knew about such things, and made preparations for the building of a suitable tomb. He frequently went to inspect the progress of the work in the company of an architect from the Engineering Section in the ministry. The architect asked him once, "Hasn't the family got an old tomb?"

"A very old one indeed," he answered, unshaken by the question. "It's become pretty crowded with so many generations of the family. There was nothing for it but to have this one built."

"There's no comparing old tombs with new ones," commented the architect. "A new tomb is a beautiful, modern structure."

"Personally I wouldn't bother to own a house in this world; a rented flat will do. But a tomb is a must, or else one's dignity is lost."

"In India they cremate the dead," the architect said, laughing.

"How awful!" Othman said with disgust.

The architect laughed again and went on: "If you want my opinion, a dead man loses dignity less by being burned than by being buried. Do you ever think about the process of decomposition that a corpse undergoes in the grave?"

"No," Othman replied with annoyance. "Nor do I want to know about it." He thought for a while and then said to the architect, "Shouldn't we provide a lavatory?"

"It will be used by strangers and made filthy."

"But surely we could plant some kind of a tree or ivy, couldn't we?"

"That won't be a problem. It could be watered from outside."

When the work had been completed, he went to examine the tomb and pay the balance. He looked over it admiringly. The door was open, and through it he could see the stairs leading down to the burial place, brightly lit by the sun. He bent forward a little to look at the floor of the tomb. It was smooth and fresh and spotlessly clean, bathed in light. He felt it was his eternal home, all ready for him; and his bones were not going to be lost in a heap of others like his parents'. Out of the depths of his soul came a soft strange voice whispering to him like a lover to lie down on the clean, bright ground, have a taste of the comforts of which he had had no share in life, and enjoy the peace which he had never experienced in the tumult of his raging emotions. For a moment he wished to obey that mysterious call and be through with the world, both its cares and its hopes.

He remained in the grip of these enigmatic thoughts until he left the cemetery and made his way back to town. And how he wished to transfer the remains of his parents to the new tomb so that he would feel more at home in it! But that, he had learned a long time ago, was not feasible, for the paupers' burial ground was so crammed with corpses, it was impossible to tell them apart.

"There's no doubt that my life today is better than it

was before," he thought, desperately trying to convince himself that he had done the right thing.

This of course did not mean that he had abandoned the path of God's eternal world, even though his zeal had noticeably waned.

THIRTY-THREE

Let the days go by!

Whatever happened, he had become a family man and the owner of a tomb; he had come to know new kinds of food, other than sheep's head, rice, lentils, and beans, and he had also discovered something to be done with money other than mummifying it in the Post Office Savings Bank.

But were days not heavy and monotonous in their passage? Had he lost hope irretrievably?

Out of the stream of days there rose, quite unexpectedly, a high and powerful tide which changed fortunes and created the world anew. One morning the whole ministry learned of the decision to appoint Bahjat Noor, the Director General, as Under Secretary of State. Thus the position of Director General became vacant for the first time in a very long period. For two weeks many hearts were beating in continuous and uneasy expectation until it was decided to promote Abdullah Wajdi, the Director of Administration, to Director General; so he became a full-fledged "Excellency." Another heart which had been tranquil for a long time began to beat with excitement.

"I'm the only eligible person," Othman said to himself. "I'm first in line for promotion and nobody has got my ability or experience. What are they going to do?"

A few weeks elapsed without anything happening. Othman spared no effort in pleading his cause with both the new Director General and the Under Secretary of State.

In a conversation, he heard someone express the opinion that the position of Director of Administration was a sensitive one. He asked him what he meant.

"It is not only experience and qualifications that count when such appointments are made. Social status matters too," said the man.

"That's only true in the case of an Under Secretary of State or a Minister," Othman retorted with indignation. "As for Director of Administration or even Director General, these are jobs open to the common people. This has been the case since British officials stopped taking them."

His anguish did not last for long, for the decision to promote him to Director of Administration was made the same month. Later he used to remember that day with a kind of passionate excitement, and he would say to himself, "The miracle took place in a twinkling!" And he would also say, "In terms of seniority there is no one now between me and the Director General."

But how did the miracle take place? He had already come to believe that he was going to be pensioned off before anybody ahead of him in the official line had moved. But a Cabinet change took place in which the Under Secretary of State was made Minister, and as a result there was that happy and unexpected shuffle lower down.

Bahjat Noor, now Under Secretary of State, said to him, "I've promoted you in the face of many objections."

Othman thanked him warmly. "But why the objections?" he inquired sadly.

"You've been too long in government service not to be able to guess the answer to your question."

However, he now set about his work with the same old vigor as in the past. He pledged before God to make history during his directorship of the administration and to create an unmatchable record full of expert and ingenious administrative practices that would last forever. He was going to demonstrate to everybody that a government post was something sacred, a duty to humanity and a form of worship in the full sense of the word.

From the first day he determined to give Abdullah Wajdi the fullest cooperation. For cooperating with the Director General was a sacred ritual of government service, and he had never been unfaithful to the duties of his office. Moreover, he was determined to use his own experience to cover up the Director General's incompetence, and even to offer him what private help he needed just as he did with the Under Secretary of State. Perhaps one day he might reap what he had sown.

"It's true that Abdullah Wajdi is still a young man," he would tell himself, "but the age of miracles has returned." But in point of fact he did not pin his hopes on miracles alone. He watched Abdullah Wajdi's corpulence with interest and listened with secret happiness to gossip about his overindulgence in food and drink.

"There is no end to the diseases that people like him are exposed to," he would think to himself.

And it was only fair, wasn't it? For in spite of his limitations, he himself was a believer, a man of God, a follower of al-Husayn, the Prophet's grandson; and God would never abandon him. On the Day of Judgment what better could a man plead than the noble ambitions he had entertained, the achievements with which he had been blessed, the steady progress he had made, and the record of the services he had done for the state and the people? The state was God's temple on earth, and our standing in both this world and the next was determined by the extent to which we exerted ourselves for its sake.

Meanwhile, the peace and quiet of his matrimonial life did not last long. However much he deceived himself and hoped for the best, the difficulties were predictable. He reproached his wife, "Qadriyya, you drink too much."

She looked at him with astonishment.

"Yes, I know, and I've always done so."

"It's never too late to overcome our bad habits," he said hopefully.

"Not worth the effort."

"But it is," he went on in the same vein, "and my hope is to see you praying and fasting. We need God's blessing."

"I believe in God," she retorted angrily. "And I know He is merciful and forgiving."

"You are a respectable woman, and a respectable woman wouldn't get drunk every night."

"How often then does a respectable woman get drunk?"

"She shouldn't at all."

She gave a hoarse laugh, and then quickly her look darkened and she said wistfully, "It's hopeless!"

"How do you mean?"

"We can't hope to have a child. It's too late."

He was conscious of sharing her sorrow but said, "We can still live happily."

She made a halfhearted attempt to keep off the drink but went on much as before. Indeed, Othman's renewed absorption in his work and her brooding about the dreadful emptiness of life without companionship may have made her an even worse addict than she already was. One evening Othman was appalled to see her taking opium.

"No!" he screamed.

"Let things be!" she said sharply.

"Since when have you been . . ." he inquired anxiously.

"Since Noah and his Flood."

"But . . ."

"Oh, lay off! It's stronger than death."

"But death and opium are one and the same."

"I don't care," came the reckless answer.

He was overcome with horror. What had he done with himself? He had gone after illusory happiness and now he had to pay the price. It was useless to think of divorce, for that would lead him into a fierce dispute which could finally destroy him.

"How do you get it?" he asked her.

She did not reply.

"So you're going to those old contacts that were always suspect. Don't you know how dangerous that can be?"

"Don't exaggerate!"

"Qadriyya, think about it, please! If you do not change your lifestyle, it will be the end of us."

To protect his reputation and his future he managed, by a great effort of will and after what nearly amounted to a fight, to get her to a rehabilitation center in Hilwan, where she stayed for a few months until her addiction was cured.

He imagined she had come back a new woman. But now food became the only consolation in her life and she ate gluttonously. She kept putting on more and more weight until her body became so grotesquely fat as to invite not just ridicule but pity. He never ceased to worry about her. All day long his attention was divided between her and his work. And he would say sadly to himself, "I have even lost the one thing that made those nights of animal behavior enjoyable, for all that's left of her now is a miserable wreck: no manners, no faith, no sense, and no taste."

He recalled the arguments which some of his politically minded colleagues advanced to justify cases like his wife's by blaming them on social injustice and class inequality. But he also recalled his own "case." Did he not grow up, like Qadriyya, poor, helpless, and deprived in every sort of way? Yes, but he discovered at the right time the divine secret in his feeble heart, just as he discovered the eternal wisdom of God and thus found the path of glory along which he walked and suffered in a manner worthy of Man, the creature of Almighty God. For this reason he hardly pitied her and again he asked, "What have I done with myself?"

What indeed was the meaning of married life without real love, a spiritual bond, the promise of posterity, or even mere human companionship? Then he addressed this warning to himself: "Take it easy! Don't let your sorrows get the better of you. You are not as strong as you used to be. There's been a new change, soft as a breeze, but cunning as a fox: it has to do with age, with the passage of time . . ."

He thought for a little while and then added: "It is Time we must thank for every achievement, and Time we must blame for every loss . . . *And nought abideth save the face of the Almighty One.*"

THIRTY-FOUR

As usual he forgot his new promotion completely. Joy disappeared and a cloud of worries built up. The duties of his Director's job soon became a familiar routine: something that he had to transcend, and quickly, for not much of life was left. Otherwise his service would come to an end while he still stood like a beggar at the door of the Blue Room. Ambition was ruthless and marriage no longer a comfort.

"God, I'm trying to guide her. In Your mercy, grant me the strength!"

But his effort was of no avail. Indeed, he had brought to her a degree of misery she could never have imagined. In the past she had been miserable, but hardly realized it; and in drink and opium she found a welcome refuge. But today she faced the void with hideous awareness, her eyes wide open and full of terror. There was nothing to console her: no love and no children.

"As a prostitute," he would say to himself, "she was a consolation to me and a pleasure, but in this comfortable home she is hell itself."

"If we each went our own way," he would also tell himself, "with a miracle I might still attain happiness. Where's my old solitude? Where?"

One evening he went back home to be greeted by bloodshot eyes and a stupefied grin.

"Have you been drinking again?" he said with horror.

She nodded with an air of resignation. "Yes, thank God!"

"And soon you'll be taking opium again too," he sighed.

"It's already happened," came the sarcastic reply.

"What do we do then?" he asked sharply.

"Everything is fine," she said calmly. "Last night I dreamed of my mother."

"I shall absolutely despair of you."

"That's all I want you to do."

He watched her as she gradually dissolved into her own world of illusions, keeping out of his way. He felt somewhat relieved, for in this way he was able to regain his solitude. And he decided, with an uneasy conscience, that this time he would let her go to pieces without opposition on his part. Addressing himself to God, he said, "Forgive me my thoughts, O God! They are part of life and therefore cruel like it."

While he was on fire with these thoughts, Radiya Abd al-Khaliq was appointed his secretary. The Head of the Personnel Office had asked him to choose a suitable secretary for himself.

"It's your right to choose your own secretary," he said. "You may even appoint a relative of yours, somebody you trust." Did the man really know nothing about his origins? Throughout his long service he had known the ingenuity of employees in digging up the most hidden secrets. It was certain that his "donkey cart" origins were no secret to anybody anymore.

"I leave the choice to you."

"You really are a model of propriety, sir," the Personnel Head flattered him.

On the following morning a young woman introduced herself to him.

"Radiya Abd al-Khaliq, Your Excellency's new secretary if you will be so kind as to approve the appointment."

"How do you do," he said, feeling gratified. "Which section do you come from?"

"Personnel."

"Fine, and what are your qualifications?"

"A B.A. in history."

He nearly asked her about her age, but he checked himself. He put her at about twenty-five. She had a remarkably good figure and her coal-dark hair flowed on either side of her long, brown face, enveloping it like a halo. Her eyes were small, clear, intelligent, and attractively bright. She had protruding incisors, sometimes considered a defect, but in her case they made her face even more attractive. Her prettiness excited him and he privately cursed the Personnel Head for his happy choice. "In this inferno of mine how I need a place of refuge!" he thought.

From the first look he took to her, perhaps driven by a secret desire for protection. And as days went by his affection for her grew even stronger, particularly when he knew that she was an orphan who lived with a spinster aunt. His inner dreams and desires were no secret to himself, but he was in no frame of mind to consider, even to consider, committing a folly.

"It's enough that I can see her face every morning," he said to himself.

The refinement of her manners, coupled with her gentle nature and the mellow look in her eyes, captivated him. All this he explained as the proper behavior of a secretary toward her boss, especially when the boss was as old as her father. But why was he thinking of her more than he should? His whole being was suffused through and through with the scent of her. He told himself that there were moments in life when those who took life seriously and those who made a joke of it were equal.

"Lord, have mercy!" he prayed.

He watched her work with interest and one day he asked her, "Do you find work in my office demanding?"

"Not at all. I love work," came the warm answer.

"So do I. Indeed, I've always done so since the day I first took up a job. And I can assure you, hard work is never wasted effort."

"But they say . . ."

"I know what they say," he interrupted her, "and I don't deny it. Favoritism . . . nepotism . . . party politics . . . preference for members of the ruling party . . . and even worse things. But efficiency is also a factor that cannot be ignored. Even incompetent people in high positions find themselves in need of someone with real talent to cover up their own inadequacy." He smiled, secretly overcome by her charm, and went on: "I have forced my way up relying on Almighty God and my work alone."

"So I've heard everywhere."

Had she? And what else had she heard? The thing that stopped Omm Zaynab, the marriage broker, from ever coming back? But that didn't matter any longer.

"I ought to tell you that I'm very pleased with your work," he said to her.

"It's all due to your kind encouragement," she said with a delighted smile.

Such purity of atmosphere was unmatchable. A purity pregnant with promise, distilling into the heart a holy joy. From such a starting point as this the lover sets out on the road that leads to happy marriage and true friendship. In this way, a man in his perplexity may stumble on situations rich with the prospect of happiness in unpropitious circumstances. The place, for instance, may be right but the time wrong: or vice versa. All this confirmed that happiness exists, but that tracks leading to it may not always be smooth. And from the interplay of time and place came either good fortune or absurdity. But you shouldn't forget mistakes either. Mistakes? Sayyida, Asila, and Onsiyya.

As days went by he would tell his heart to beware. As usual, he started to fear Radiya as much as he liked her. And as usual too, he surrendered himself to the current and waited for life's course to be determined by an unknown destiny.

THIRTY-FIVE

As the days passed by, compounded of work in the office and wretchedness at home, secret longings took fire in his heart. It appeared that the universe had come to a standstill and that Abdullah Wajdi had become as immovable in the position of Director General as the Great Pyramid.

"There isn't a flicker of hope!" he thought.

How would the miracle happen this time? There he was with only a few black hairs remaining in his head: his eyesight was now poor and he had to wear glasses, his digestive system had lost its usual rigor so that he had to use drugs for the first time in his life, and his back had grown humped from years of bending over a desk and taking no exercise.

"I'm still strong, thank God!" he would say to himself. And he would spend a long time looking at himself in the mirror, which was not his habit, and thinking, "I still look all right!"

At that time he had written a comprehensive book on employment regulations which caused a sensation in official circles. Despite his advancing age he continued to slave away both at his office work and on his translations —partly because he enjoyed it and partly as an escape from the burden of his marital life on the one hand and his emotional excitement, reckless and frivolous as he thought it, on the other.

"There's no denying that the hour I spend with her looking at the mail every morning is my share of happiness!"

The exchange of greetings and smiles. Comments on work. Disguised flirtation. Discreet compliments on her hairstyle, her shoes, or her blouse. On one occasion he was admiring her hairstyle when she said, "I'm thinking of having it cut short."

"No, no!" he protested.

She smiled at the warmth of his protest over something quite unconnected with administrative statutes.

"But . . ."

"Leave it as it is!" he interrupted.

"But the fashion . . ."

"I know nothing about the fashion, but I like it the way it is."

She blushed. He studied her carefully but found no trace of displeasure in her face. He decided to put to use the lessons he had learned during the happier moments of his past. So one morning he presented her with a handsome little case. Radiya was taken aback.

"What's that?" she asked.

"A small thing for a great occasion!"

"But . . . but how did you know?"

"Many happy returns."

"In point of fact it really *is* my birthday."

"Of course it is."

"But . . . you're so kind . . . I don't deserve . . ."

"Say no more! With you, silence is more expressive!"

"I'm really grateful."

"And I'm really happy!"

He sighed, gathered his strength, and then surrendered completely to his emotions. Without further thought he burst out, passionately and in dead earnest, "What can I do? I'm in love!"

She looked down, accepting his confession and happily surrendering to whatever it should bring.

"It is the last thing I ought to speak about," he went on, "but what can I do?"

Her brown face flushed darker, but she stayed where she was sitting submissively as if waiting for more.

"I'm not a young man, as you see." He was quiet for a long while and then went on: "And I'm married." What was it he wanted? Perhaps what he didn't want was to face the possibility of failure or in the end death, all alone; without the warmth of love and without children.

"But what can I do?" he said again. "I'm in love."

Silence reigned again. Nothing mattered any longer and he asked her almost jokingly, "What do you say to that?"

She smiled and mumbled something indistinct.

"Maybe you think I'm selfish?"

"No, I don't," she whispered.

"Or senile?"

She laughed softly and answered, "Don't do yourself an injustice!"

"What you say is very kind but what shall we do?" For the third time there was silence.

"I really do want to know what you think," he said again.

"It's a delicate situation and rather bewildering," she said gravely. "And I don't like to be inhuman or cruel."

"Are you hinting at my wife?"

"That's something you surely must consider."

"Leave that to me, it's my responsibility."

"Very well."

"But I want to know what you think apart from that."

She was now in much better control of her emotions and said, "Haven't I already made that clear in what I've been saying?"

"I'm so happy, Radiya, to hear that ... It shows that my love for you has your blessing."

"Yes, it does," she said without hesitation. He was drunk with rapture.

"I don't mind what happens now!" he said with royal abandon, and then added in a voice that pleaded for sympathy: "I must tell you that I have never known happiness."

"Can that really be so?"

"I've had a difficult life and a miserable marriage!"

"You never gave me that impression."

"How so?"

"You have always seemed such a wise person to me, and it's my belief that wise people are happy people."

"What an idea!"

"I'm sorry."

"But your love makes me happy."

He believed he had won the greatest prize of his life and that next to the power of almighty God, the power of love was the greatest.

Later on he went with her to her place in al-Sayyida Zaynab. She introduced him to her old spinster aunt. From the beginning it was obvious to him that the woman was not in favor of the marriage and she made her feelings only too clear. The matter was discussed from all aspects.

"Divorce your wife first!" she said.

But he rejected the idea, explaining apologetically that his wife "was ill."

"You are an old man and an untrustworthy one," she blurted out sharply.

Radiya rushed to his defense.

"Don't be cross with my aunt!" she said.

"What do you propose to do?" asked the aunt after a while.

"I want our marriage to remain secret for a short period until the time is suitable to make it public."

"Well, that's a fine story, I must say!" cried the aunt. "And what do you think of that?" she asked, turning to Radiya.

"It's something we have agreed on. I'm not very happy about it, but I haven't turned it down."

"Do as you please!" she shouted at her. "But the whole thing seems to me wicked and sinful."

"Aunt!" screamed the girl.

"Are you trying to take advantage of us because we're poor and have got no one to protect us?" said the aunt angrily, turning on Othman.

"I've known poverty and loneliness more than anyone," retorted Othman, feeling exasperated for the first time.

"Then let each of you go your own way," answered the aunt imploringly.

"We've already made up our minds to stay together," came Radiya's adamant reply.

"What can I do? God's will be done!"

One month later the marriage took place in the aunt's house. They bought furniture to suit their new life. Othman said to himself that life was a series of dreams and nightmares and that his last dream was the happiest of all. He would stay in Radiya's flat until about midnight and then go back to Rawd al-Faraj, where Qadriyya, lost in her own world, never asked him where he had been or what he had been doing. Wisely he decided to postpone having children until he had made the marriage public, so that his new wife would not find herself in an embarrassing situation at the office.

In his overwhelming happiness he forgot how old he was and how totally bogged down were his hopes for the Director General's position; and he forgot Qadriyya. He told himself that life had only been created as a stage for the performance of the wonders of Providence.

THIRTY-SIX

For the first time in his life he was seen striding about in handsome clothes: a gray suit made of English wool and English shoes too. As for his shirts and ties, Radiya had chosen them herself. For the first time too he used eau de cologne and shaved every day, and if he had not been too shy he would have dyed his hair. And again for the first time he took vitamins, and he looked after his health and cleanliness more than he had ever done in the past. He said to Radiya, "With you, my darling, I will begin a new life, new in the full sense of the word." He kissed her and went on: "We shall have children . . ." He paused for a long while and then continued: "Nobody knows when his time will be up, but I come from a long-lived family. May God give us long life!"

Radiya kissed him and said, "My heart tells me we'll have a happy future."

"The heart of a believer is his guide! I've got enough faith to make up for a multitude of sins and I've served the state with enough devotion to atone for many transgressions; and when things have settled down, I will go on the pilgrimage to be reborn, soul and body."

As for Qadriyya, she was steadily going downhill, and this relieved him altogether of responsibility for her. He was not without sympathy for her but he remained afraid of telling her about his second marriage.

He did not forget that he was approaching the end of his service with no real hope of attaining his life's most treasured dream. But as the days went rapidly past, something unexpected took place. Abdullah Wajdi was appointed Under Secretary of State for Foreign Affairs, so all of a sudden Othman saw the Director General's post vacant in front of him. He closed his eyes and tried to master the beating of his heart. With the vacant post occupying the foreground, everything else in his life—his bride, his joys, his hopes—was consigned to oblivion. His suppressed ambition exploded and once again he worshipped in the sacred temple of advancement.

Radiya said to him, "Everybody is talking about you as the only candidate."

"God grant our hopes come true," he said piously, and went on in an air of genteel thanksgiving: "Isn't life amazing? In just one moment it wipes away sorrows that the oceans themselves could not wash off. A kind mother, that's what life is, though sometimes she treats us cruelly."

Othman went without delay to the Foreign Office to congratulate Abdullah Wajdi. The latter welcomed him.

"Let me confess to you, Mr. Bayyumi, that I was doubly gratified," he said courteously. "Once at my own appointment as Under Secretary, and once because I knew for sure you would replace me at the ministry."

Othman left the Foreign Office intoxicated with happiness. He wondered whether they would first appoint him Acting Director General and then give him substantive promotion or let him stay where he was until he was promoted. Every day of waiting was a torment. Suffer indeed he did, despite his knowledge that the Minister had a good opinion of him and that he was the special protégé of the Under Secretary of State. When his patience had been exhausted he went to see Bahjat Noor, the Under Secretary of State. The man gave him a warm welcome as he said, "It's as though I read your thoughts."

Othman smiled in confusion and was lost for words.

"But you do not read my thoughts," the man went on.

"I owe to you everything good in my life," Othman answered pensively.

"A little patience is all I ask of you," the Under Secretary of State said, smiling. "I trust I will have good news to tell you in the end."

Othman left the man's office feeling grateful but wondering why he had asked him to be patient. He told himself that the omens were good but even so he did not feel completely secure. Patiently he suffered. After one week the Under Secretary of State called him to his office. Othman thought he read a cool look in the man's eyes and his heart pounded.

Bahjat Noor said, "You're probably wondering why your promotion has been delayed."

"Indeed I am, Your Excellency."

"Well, you know my opinion of you and I may tell you that the Minister's opinion is the same as mine."

"I'm most gratified."

The Under Secretary of State was silent. They looked at each other for a long while.

"What do you deduce from this?" the great man asked.

"That there must be objections from above?" Othman answered, feeling very low.

"Frankly there's a bit of a battle going on."

"And the outcome, Your Excellency?"

"I don't think the Minister will give in."

"How much hope do you think there is?" he asked, feeling his mouth go dry.

"Oh, plenty! Just put your trust in God like the devout believer you are."

His trust in God was boundless, but the devil had long been active in the department. Othman was constantly having to cross a bridge of nails.

"There's little chance left," he sighed.

"Don't be sad!" said Radiya. "Promotion is not the only thing in life to look forward to."

But sad he was, and his sadness settled deep in his heart. He aged, as it were, by a whole generation and all life's dreams turned to ashes. Radiya suggested that they spend a day the following weekend in al-Qanatir Gardens. He welcomed the idea and let her lead him away to wander with her in the huge park. She was the only happy thing in his whole life.

"People have always forgotten their worries in nature's arms," she said, laughing.

She squatted on the grass and gave herself up, soul and body, to the water, the green lawns, and the cloud-dotted sky. He watched her with admiration and warmly endorsed what she said about the beauties of nature. But when he looked around all he saw was scenery that had never meant anything to him in the past; nor did it now. The fact was, he was always absorbed in an inner world, a world of restricted thoughts and fancies conjured up by instinct, a world in which God and God's earthly glory,

187

and the conflict between good and evil, predominated. These things apart, he saw nothing of life.

"Surely you love nature!"

"I love you."

"Look at these happy couples all around us!"

"Yes, there are so many of them!"

She rested her palm on his hand as she said, "Let's forget our worries, it's so refreshing here."

"Yes, let's!"

"But you're so sad."

He sighed without speaking.

"Look," she said, "you are a senior official in grade one. Others would be happy with much less than that." He nearly told her that true faith was the contrary of trivial happiness.

"I'm not like other officials, and to prevent me from occupying the position I deserve is despicable behavior and a blatant breach of the moral system the state operates on."

"Don't you think you set too high a value on government positions?"

"A government position is a brick in the edifice of the state, and the state is an exhalation of the spirit of God, incarnate on earth."

She gazed at him with amazement and he realized that she did not comprehend the nature of his faith and all it comprised.

"That's a new idea to me," she said. "But I've often heard that the spirit of the people comes from the spirit of God."

He smiled scornfully. "Don't speak to me about political conflicts!"

"But that's the real life."

"What absolute rubbish!"

"But the whole world . . ."

"The real world," he interrupted her, "is in the depths of the heart." His heart ached at the thought that she might think he was mad, as some idiots did, and he said to her, seeking a way out, "Let's not argue!"

She gave way and smiled sweetly.

"It's time," he went on, seeking refuge in a new hope, "to make our marriage public."

She blushed. "Is our way clear now?"

"We must face life with courage to be worthy of happiness."

"How beautiful to hear you say that!"

"I'm going to tell my wife." His face brightened with a smile. "A sacred power calls on me to start life afresh and father children I can be proud of."

THIRTY-SEVEN

He declared his good intentions again in the presence of Radiya's aunt.

"For the first time you appear to be a sensible man," said the old woman.

Both Othman and Radiya laughed.

"Our life is worth nothing without you, Aunt," he said.

The old woman showed her approval with a smile.

"We've spent a good day in al-Qanatir Gardens and it's time for me to go," he said.

"Will you tell your wife tonight?" asked the aunt.

"The sooner, the better!" he answered as he got up. He took one step forward and then stopped, his expression visibly changing.

"What's the matter?" Radiya asked.

He pointed at his chest without uttering a word.

"Do you feel tired? Sit down!"

"A severe pain here!" he mumbled, indicating his chest again.

She rushed forward to help him but he fell back into his chair and fainted.

When he came to he found himself lying in bed, his clothes still on except for his tie and shoes. He saw in the room a new person, who, despite his weakness, he realized was a doctor. Radiya's face was sad and drained of color and even her aunt's face wore an expression of dejection.

"How do you feel?" asked the doctor as he looked into his eyes.

"What's happened?" answered Othman.

"Nothing very serious."

"But ..."

"But you will need quite a long rest."

"I feel perfectly all right," said Othman, greatly disturbed. "I think I can get up."

"If that's the case, I must tell you that your condition is critical," the doctor said firmly. "In medical terms it is not serious, but any failure to do what I tell you can make it so. You need complete rest for at least a month."

"A month!" exclaimed Othman.

"You must take the treatment regularly, and rigidly follow the prescribed diet. This is no matter for argument. I will look in again tomorrow." He put his instruments back in his bag and added: "Make sure you remember every word I've said!"

The doctor went out, Othman's eyes pursuing him with a look of anger and despair. Radiya came nearer until she was standing next to the bed. She stared at him and smiled encouragingly.

"A little patience and everything will be all right." The look on his face reflected his anxiety. Tenderly she touched his forehead with the tips of her fingers.

"Don't worry! You'll be fine."

"But there are so many things ..."

"I will take care of the situation at the ministry."

"How?"

"The truth must be known. There's nothing wrong with that."

"What a situation!"

"Your wife must know too."

"That's even harder."

"We must face reality at any cost."

"You just rest!" Radiya's aunt interrupted.

Radiya was right. He mustn't give up. The will to live in him rejected despair and surrender, come what might! In the end the whole thing was something of a joke.

He shut his eyes, and let events outside weave their way as if they had nothing to do with him, though he was in fact their very center. His colleagues in the office soon came to see him, and as he was not allowed to receive visitors, he was flooded with dozens of get-well cards. He read the prayers and good wishes they contained and remembered Sa'fan Basyuni and Hamza al-Suwayfi. His thoughts reverted to memories which made him feel uneasy. He wondered how Hamza al-Suwayfi was and whether he was still alive. Then he reflected that new employees who did not know him, and who probably would not have a chance to, were joining the department now. And overhead, above all this, clouds raced in the sky and vanished beyond the horizon. Only now did he understand the meaning of the movement of the sun.

He closed his eyes for a while and then opened them to find Qadriyya sitting near the bed gazing at him. In her eyes he saw a stupefied look, soft, dark, and indifferent, like the moon when veiled with a transparent cloud. He realized she no longer lived in this world and was not to be feared. However, she seemed to have been told to be nice to him, for she asked him calmly, "How do you feel?"

He smiled in confusion and gratefully murmured, "Fine, thank you."

"They told me that moving you to your 'original' home might be dangerous," she said, as though reproaching the unknown. "I would have liked to look after you."

"Thank you, Qadriyya. You've always been so good to me."

"You must rest until God helps you out of your illness." She shook her head with an air of wisdom that was not typical of her and went on: "I don't blame you. I understand everything. You want a son, and you're right. God grant you your wish!"

"You are so good and kind, Qadriyya."

She relapsed into silence and was then transported into a world of her own suffused with the perfumes of Paradise. He felt deeply relieved because the secret was out, and the critical and potentially explosive moment had passed. On the other hand, he fully realized the meaning of his illness. What hope was there now of promotion? And . . . and what hope was there of having children?

"I didn't have the slightest warning," he said to Radiya.

"The doctor wasn't surprised."

"This has certainly taught me what it means to be taken unawares."

"It's only a passing cloud."

"I'm very sorry for you, I really am."

"Me? All I care about is your health and well-being."

He looked at her with affection. "One can never tell what's going to happen to one in this world."

She bowed her head in silence till he feared she was seeking to hide a tear.

"I'm grateful to you," he said. "You are a spark of light in this world of ours, which has no logic and no real existence."

"Look on the bright side of life, for your sake and mine!"

He sighed. "Has Qadriyya gone in peace?"

"Yes."

"I thought I heard her voice rend the air. What was the matter?"

"Nothing at all. She's an unlucky woman."

"Yes. One makes mistakes as often as one breathes."

"You must rest completely."

He looked at her tenderly. "Will we be able to realize one of our hopes?"

"Yes, with God's help."

He stared at her sadly. "In a moment of despair I put the thought of promotion behind me and all my hopes centered on a single dream—a child."

"We shall have one."

"Thank you, darling."

"You just take it easy and everything will be fine."

"But how could a hope of immortal kind be lost? It would mean that the annihilation of the world is possible and may, quite simply, happen . . ."

"Wouldn't it be better to keep philosophy for another time?"

"Very well."

"Is there anything you want before you sleep?"

"Just to know the secret of existence," he answered with a smile.

THIRTY-EIGHT

At last he was able to receive his visitors. Everybody came
to see him: his colleagues, the staff working under him,
and even porters and messengers. Gatherings took place
in the bedroom, lasted a long time, and seemed to promise
full recovery. Conversations went on about health and illness, miraculous recoveries, and the mercy of God. They
also discussed the skill of doctors, the news of the ministry
and the department, the cards sent by the Minister and the
Under Secretary of State.

"Why didn't the Under Secretary come himself?"

"He's been up to his neck in work. Still, he has no excuse."

"Well, and what does that matter?"

Soon conversations turned to public affairs: the latest
radio concert, prices, the generation gap, etc.

Othman took some part in the conversation, but mostly
he just listened, and suddenly he found them discussing
politics. Once again talk about the conflict raging in society and the slogans that go with it resounded in his ears:
freedom, democracy, the people, the working masses, revolutionary ideologies, and confident predictions about the
upheavals of tomorrow.

He told himself that every individual staggered under
the weight of his own ambitions: was that not enough?
But they believed that each man's hopes were dependent

on his dreams of revolution. Well! What revolution could guarantee *him* recovery, a child, and the fulfillment of God's word in the sacred state? But he kept his thoughts secret. They were a paltry flock, grazing in the pastures of misery. They hung their hopes on dreams because their faith was weak and they did not know that solitude was an act of worship.

A feeling of warmth generated by the assurance of imminent recovery made him want to try his strength. Being on his own in the room was a good opportunity, so he moved slowly to the edge of the bed and lowered his legs carefully until his feet touched the floor.

"My trust is in God," he mumbled.

He stood up and leaned against the bed until he gained confidence in himself, then he moved his feet tentatively like a child taking its first steps on its own. His legs barely supported him, so weak was he, and so long had he been on his back. He walked till he reached the door. He opened it and continued to walk in the direction of the living room. He wanted to give Radiya and her aunt a pleasant surprise. As he approached the room, he heard voices: an argument between Radiya and her aunt.

"Who? Who?" Radiya was asking sharply.

Uncharacteristically the aunt answered in soft tones, "You've brought it all on yourself. I warned you long ago."

"What's the use now?"

"See what your greed and miscalculation have brought you!"

"Go ahead and shout so he will hear you!"

Then they fell silent.

He returned to his bed stunned. What were they arguing about? What was it she had brought on herself? What greed? What miscalculation? He closed his eyes and bit his lip.

"O God! What does that mean? Could it be true?" Why shouldn't it? He himself had always wanted to play that game, but had been unlucky. So strong was his feeling of frustration he was completely carried away with it.

"What a fool I have been!"

He had a setback, suffering a further attack. For days life and death fought over him. He appeared determined to cling to life despite everything and despite telling himself it would be a long and losing battle.

"God's will be done!" he said.

People said he had passed the critical stage, but it was known from the beginning that he would have to stay in bed indefinitely. He revealed his secret to nobody. When Radiya came in he kept his eyes closed. He bore her no grudge nor was he angry with her.

"I have no right to hate her more than I hate myself," he would tell himself.

"If one day I can have a child by her, I will not hesitate, so the game of life will have its bright side as well as its dark," he thought. And in the end he sighed. "What a fool I was! What a bad end I have come to!" He was not angry but he no longer had any confidence in space.

One evening Radiya entered the room, her face flushed.

"The Under Secretary of State has come to visit you," she said.

Bahjat Noor came in with his usual dignified bearing. He shook his hand and sat down as he said, "You look marvelous!"

Othman was touched. "This is a great honor, Your Excellency."

"You deserve to be honored. Good services cannot be forgotten."

Tears came to his eyes.

"Your absence has created a vacuum that nobody else can fill," said the Under Secretary.

"You're so kind ... That's why you say these things ..."

"Soon you'll be all right and you'll come back to us. I have brought you good news." The man smiled while Othman gazed at him with incomprehension.

"A decision has been made today to promote you to the position of Director General." Othman continued to gaze at him blankly.

"Right and justice have won in the end."

"I owe everything to your kindness," murmured Othman.

"His Excellency the Minister has asked me to convey to you his best wishes for a speedy recovery."

"I'm most grateful to His Excellency."

The man went away, leaving him in the seventh heaven, as though he had been a messenger of mercy sent by the unknown. Othman received the congratulations of Radiya and her aunt with his eyes shut. And again he felt he no longer had any confidence in space.

"How happy I am!" he heard her say.

He savored his success tranquilly. He was now "His

Excellency," the occupant of the Blue Room, the authority on legal rulings and administrative directives, the inspiration behind perceptive instructions for wise administration and the efficient manipulation of people's interests, one of God's faithful empowered to do good and prevent evil.

"My cup shall be full, O Lord," he addressed himself to God, "the day I am enabled by Your gracious mercy to get up and exercise power and exalt Your word on earth."

But the doctor said to him, "What matters to me is your health, not your job." Indeed, the doctor was unbendingly obdurate, and if his prognosis proved correct, that promotion would never take effect.

"Health alone is not enough to make a true believer happy," Othman said to him.

"I've never heard *that* before."

"If I use up my sick-leave entitlement, I'll be pensioned off."

"Well, there's nothing we can do about that."

Othman was depressed and he thought to himself, "Perhaps they only promoted me as an act of charity, knowing all the time that I would not be able to take up the job."

He called Radiya and said to her, "I don't want to trouble you any more."

She was puzzled. "How do you mean?"

"Nursing a sick man is a horrible business."

Radiya protested again but he was determined. He discussed the idea with his doctor, who agreed and arranged for him to be moved to a private room in the hospital. Visitors apart, he had reverted to his old solitude.

Days went by in their endless progression. He was almost cut off from the outside world. Qadriyya too stopped visiting him, her condition having gotten worse. He resigned himself to his fate and he no longer bothered about the past, the present, or the future. He tolerated the hours Radiya spent by his side with extreme irritation but kept his sorrows to himself, believing them at the same time to be merited. His staunch faith in the sanctity of his convictions, in the harshness and holiness of life, the struggle and the agony, and the faraway and exalted hope, all remained unshaken. And he said to himself that occasional failure to achieve one's aspirations did not undermine one's belief in them. Not even illness or death itself could do so; for all that was noble and meaningful in life came from one's determination to pursue them.

Empty words of encouragement were hateful to him, and he resigned himself to the fact that taking up his new position was a dream. He was also resigned to the fact that fathering children was another dream. Yet, who knew?

What hurt him most was that everything went on without any attention being paid to him: appointments, promotions, and pensionings, love, marriage, and even divorce, political conflicts and their feverish slogans, the succession of day and night . . .

Down there, he could hear the cries of hawkers announcing the approach of winter.

Maybe it was as well that the new tomb out there in the sunlight had given him such pleasure.

The leading Arabic novelist, Naguib Mahfouz was born in Cairo in 1911 and began writing when he was seventeen. A student of philosophy and an avid reader, he has been influenced by many Western writers, he says, including Flaubert, Zola, Camus, Dostoyevsky, and above all, Proust. Until his retirement in 1972, Mahfouz worked in various government ministries—but he was always writing. Today he has more than thirty novels to his credit, among them his masterwork *The Cairo Trilogy*. He lives in the Cairo suburb of Agouza with his wife and two daughters.